Books by L.A. Kennedy

The Genesys Project

Immortal Amour
Dark Amour
Wicked Amour

I0620736

Wicked Amour

ISBN # 978-1-78686-041-5

©Copyright L.A. Kennedy 2016

Cover Art by Posh Gosh ©Copyright 2016

Interior text design by Claire Siemaszkiewicz

Totally Bound Publishing

This is a work of fiction. All characters, places and events are from the author's imagination and should not be confused with fact. Any resemblance to persons, living or dead, events or places is purely coincidental.

All rights reserved. No part of this publication may be reproduced in any material form, whether by printing, photocopying, scanning or otherwise without the written permission of the publisher, Totally Bound Publishing.

Applications should be addressed in the first instance, in writing, to Totally Bound Publishing. Unauthorised or restricted acts in relation to this publication may result in civil proceedings and/or criminal prosecution.

The author and illustrator have asserted their respective rights under the Copyright Designs and Patents Acts 1988 (as amended) to be identified as the author of this book and illustrator of the artwork.

Published in 2016 by Totally Bound Publishing, Newland House, The Point, Weaver Road, Lincoln, LN6 3QN, United Kingdom.

No part of this book may be reproduced, scanned, or distributed in any printed or electronic form without permission. Please do not participate in or encourage piracy of copyrighted materials in violation of the authors' rights. Purchase only authorised copies.

Totally Bound Publishing is a subsidiary of Totally Entwined Group Limited.

If you purchased this book without a cover you should be aware that this book is stolen property. It was reported as "unsold and destroyed" to the publisher and neither the author nor the publisher has received any payment for this "stripped book".

The Genesys Project

WICKED AMOUR

L.A. KENNEDY

Dedication

Dedicated to Miss Paula. It all started with a poke in the eye. Funny how things work out. Thank you for every phone call and agreement that boys were awful. *I may have been wrong on that one.* When the world becomes dark and scary, thank you for reminding me that I am never alone and you are always there with me.

And for Van, in Sloan's song "Money City Maniacs," I swear I'm hearing something entirely different. *You'll never listen to that song the same way again. You're welcome.* Thank you for being my sounding board, shoulder to lean on and walking, talking dictionary. You're probably one of the coolest people I know.

Acknowledgements

A huge thank you goes to Jamie Rose, my amazing and remarkable editor. Thank you for all you do and have done for me. Thank you for your endless guidance and support. Your eye for detail and hours upon hours of dedication have helped bring this series to life!

To the talented Emmy, thank you for your magic. Thank you to the rest of the team at TEG. You're an incredible group of people!

"Writing isn't about making money, getting famous, getting dates, getting laid, or making friends. In the end, it's about enriching the lives of those who will read your work, and enriching your own life, as well." — Stephen King

A special thank you to my readers, writer friends and family. None of this would be possible without you all. From the bottom of my heart, thank you for enriching my life.

Let your plans be dark and impenetrable as night,
And when you move, fall like a thunderbolt.
— Sun Tzu, *The Art of War*

Prologue

Death comes to those who are deserving of its mercy. It cradles the worthy and brings them home to Elysium. Death is not cold. It is the warm comfort that comes when it's earned. It is life that is unforgiving and brutal, murderously cold and hateful.

Life takes everything from a person then leaves him spinning out of control, gripping at the thorns it has shoved down his throat to silence him. Death is the only way out of this demanding circle of sorrow, for those who are lucky enough to taste that clemency.

Riam was not one of those lucky few. For him, death would never come to his open arms and begging bones.

Riam—who was never given a last name—fell to his knees, crying out at the carnage. A battle that had taken but minutes to start and end had slaughtered hundreds of souls he'd never laid eyes on—that is, until the moment he robbed them of their lives. A field that had once been lush and green was ground zero for death and destruction—an entire people removed from the face of the planet. Their only crime was that a Seer had caught them in his sights and viewed what their race would do for generations to come.

Riam and his people were Seers—hybrid children from the line of a Sibyl, an oracle. They were half Vampyre and half Sibyl, cursed to live for centuries. Through supernatural insight passed down their line, they could see the past, present and future. They used that sight to start and end wars before the very whisper of a battle could be heard. Their interruptions on written paths would later damn mankind. They had changed the roads man walked down and altered their outcomes, in hopes of saving humanity. In the end, they had saved no one.

The field he knelt in would soon be forgotten. The men and women who had perished — taken by Riam and his people — would become the dust that formed the hills for the next generation to come. The screams of the fallen still echoed in Riam's ears, as he stared down at his sister, Layla, who had fought beside him.

Layla stared up at the stars, suffering from a mortal wound. The attacker had landed the only killing blow for her kind with an immortal body. This was her second life, the last death. Her first death had given her a life governed by the sun and moon. With a wooden spike jutting out of her chest, he knew this was the end of her existence. Riam clung to her blood-soaked hand. He was torn between wanting her to live and allowing her the mercy of a warrior's death, an honorable ending.

He brushed Layla's hair from her eyes. The white strands were highlighted with blood from dozens of people who'd fought to live and failed. The human warriors' ability to fight wasn't nearly as strong as two dozen Seers determined to cleanse humanity of those they saw fit. The Seers were the first to commit genocide. They were its creator. They were blind to the unspoken rule — nothing in life was free — and now they all would pay. No one spoke of this. And the end result in years to come would be catastrophic.

Layla's eyes rolled to the side, her focus landing on Riam. "Brother, let me go. I am done. I want to go home to the warm arms of Elysium. You are the last of our father's line now. Do *not* leave this as our story. There has been enough death, enough blinding war. Leave this place. This is not why we were created. This is not who you are. Please, brother of mine, I beg of you to leave this life. There is no honor to be found here."

Riam squeezed her hand and nodded. He hadn't said it out loud before, but he agreed. He was done with this, done with the killing. Thousands of people had died at their hands for a cause he no longer believed in. There weren't many of them left who still trusted their ways. They no longer led their people to victory. They followed like scared sheep. They killed because they were told to. His people feared a life where they didn't have spoken purpose and a calling. They were afraid of being out in the world, living without dictation. Individuality was not something taught to his people. *All for one or nothing at all.*

"Swear to me, Riam. Swear you will put down your sword and leave this place. Give me your word of honor. You will close this chapter in your book and go forward, never to look back again. I cannot leave this world unless I know you will live, truly live, Riam. This is *not* living. This is death, nothing more. We don't have the right to do this to mankind. We were created to remove the darkness, not become it. All we have done is bring shame upon our names."

Riam sighed and closed his eyes. Hot tears rolled down his cheeks. "I give you my word."

Layla rolled her head back to the sky and smiled. Breathing out one last breath. "I love you, Riam. I'm going home."

Riam held his sister's hand as she died her final death. The pain in his chest vibrated throughout his limbs, sending tingles to his fingertips. He breathed deeply, keeping himself from screaming. The tears poured slowly as he prayed for his sister's safe return to Elysium. With the knowledge that she would soon be home in the arms of the Orygin and his fallen family, he was able to let her go.

"Riam." A hand touched his shoulder. He recognized the voice of their leader, Myranda, their Aegys, spoken softly to his right.

"Myranda. I cannot do this anymore, Aegys," Riam whispered. He turned and hung his head, still kneeling in the warm, blood-soaked earth. The feet of his Aegys, soaked into the red gore to her ankles, stood in front of him.

"Riam, our calling is a brutal one, but it is our burden to carry for the hope of mankind," she said. Her voice was soft, yet commanding. She could encourage an entire army with meaningless words strung together. She was one of the last true believers in their cause.

"We are missionaries, Aegys, not murderers," Riam said, lifting his head. She stood with her shoulders back and a look of pride on her face. The look disgusted Riam. He pointed to the field of fallen souls. "This is war. This is murder. Our actions are disrupting the natural destiny of mankind. We took a vow to allow the natural flow of life to continue, acting only as fate dictates. But I can't see our paths anymore. It is all lost to me. Our wicked intentions have altered the future in such a way that I no longer have the sight. A Seer without sight is a Seer on the wrong path."

Riam stood, looking over the field once more. At his feet lay the final straw, the death of his sister and of his fellow man. He was done. His soul could no longer continue to fight. He dropped his sword and shield, hearing it mush into the soaked grass. Turning his back on his Aegys, he did what he never thought he would do. He deserted her.

Riam walked away from the last remaining tie to his bloodline, his sister. He'd watched eleven of his siblings die at the hands of this cause. He'd held his brothers and sisters as they'd left this world of war. But he'd never held the hand of anyone he was closer to than his sister. He had no one left. He had his people, but he knew he couldn't remain. He was now completely alone.

It would be the last time Riam saw his people. It was the bloody end of standing shoulder to shoulder in the trenches.

Over the years to come, other Seers would follow suit. The Seers disbanded, coming to the same conclusion as Riam. They had changed the future based on what they'd thought was right. A future once seen clearly had become clouded and unseen. Their wicked ways had altered the future too greatly for any prophet or oracle to see. Their changes had killed more than what was originally written, and they had saved people who weren't meant to live. Those people went on to slaughter hundreds.

When Riam regained his sight, he saw a future that carried death and chaos. The Seers had unknowingly helped unleash two sides, darkness and light. Their meddling would be the undoing of mankind.

Dismantled, the Seers left their old traditions behind them, all swearing never to dabble in forced change again. Destiny would not be challenged and fate would not be derailed anymore. They had opened a door they could never close. They'd helped create the seed of the Rancor Order. They had been the first straw, the first reason for the Genesys to push forward and birth children.

Chapter One

Present day

People didn't need water to drown or flames to burn. They drowned in lost hope. They drowned when they'd gulped down too much desperation and had traded acts of love for wickedness. The evil that had been birthed from wicked decisions and wrong-turned paths licked flames up their legs and burned them alive.

Riam knew all too well what wicked decisions could do. He and his people had created a future that all of mankind was paying for now.

Riam faced north in his bedroom, in his usual cross-legged *Sukhasana* yoga pose, with a thick ring of salt surrounding him, and he meditated. Meditation pulled his guard down, the salt kept the noise of the wicked from ringing in his ears. Although he was not Wiccan and did not practice ritual magick, he knew evil existed and it gunned for him as much as he had gunned for it. Millennia of hunting the dark and perverted had left his name tattooed at the top of every evil and corrupt hit list in town. He was used to having the massive target on his head. Every path taken had a price and he paid dearly, always. It was a debt he was more than willing to pay, for the safety of those he cared about.

He sat with his long sandy-blond hair pulled up into a bun. His body was nude and free of any objects that grounded him to his current reality. He focused on letting go of his thoughts, willing himself to let go of the world that surrounded him. He cleared his mind of those in the house, of the noises that echoed down the halls, from the pool balls that cracked against one another to the playful banter that passed between his fellow Slayers. He had built a wall in his mind and around his body to filter out the sounds of the world. It left him alone and in silence. He directed his thoughts inward on his center-most consciousness, releasing the external world and the distractions it brought with it.

It had become increasingly difficult to calm his thoughts after the raid six months ago. Flashes of war had filled his mind and busied his thoughts — war from a time so long ago that the memories had bled into one another to form one large tribute to the man he used to be. He once had been a man who was brave, fearless and a warrior of the highest rank — someone he was thankful to have walled up in a stone tower in the back of his mind, never to escape again. He'd become a man who couldn't look in the mirror. To do so would mean he'd have to look deep into himself — a task that was much harder than any time he'd stood alone on a battlefield and faced off against dozens of enemies.

Everyone struggled with looking Riam in the eyes. He didn't blame them. The darkness of his soul would stare out and scare even the strongest. For Riam, it was a constant reminder of how close he had come to the brink of Hades. His actions had paved the way toward his own personal pit of hell, a cliff he looked over each time the thought of screwing with fate had crossed his mind.

In the six months that had passed, between the cleansing of Blood Alley and this moment he now sat in, nothing had changed and yet everything was transformed. Their raid had knocked the Rancor Order on their asses. Fewer and fewer hunts were needed. Although the Order was in hiding, the Slayers still went after them. And as they'd slaughtered the Order, no one had heard from Strain. He'd dropped off the face of the earth. The Slayers knew that he'd be back. Cockroaches always came back for the decaying leftovers and unwanted odds and ends. And that was Strain—a scavenger of the lowest variety.

Even with Strain in hiding, the Genesys was still out there. This war would continue until he was gone and his ashes were scattered across six bodies of water. The Genesys would continue building an empire with or without his son. Until he was stopped, the Slayers would continue their hunt for his ending.

The cleansing had wiped out the Proletaryans and the labs needed to create them. The raid had destroyed the compounds, training camps, caches and stockpiles. The incursion against evil had done what it had promised it would do, bring Hades to the doorsteps of the scum that tainted the streets of Van City. Each door Riam had kicked down, he'd hoped to find one specific woman—the woman who had screamed for him to leave her behind. The woman he'd left the night they'd saved Neri, Zylan's Fyrvor. He didn't regret the choice. Neri had to be saved. She was needed to create a cure for the irregular gene. Regret or no regret, it still pained him to have left the woman behind.

'*Get out of here.*'

Riam could still hear the woman behind the door who'd screamed to him.

A little window in the door had showed the smallest slice of who she was, but it was enough to burn the image of her eyes into his mind. She'd stood with shoulders straight, nude body bruised and battered and not a drop of fear in her voice. Her voice had rolled over his skin like a million ants marching. It held determination and fearlessness he could relate to. The smell of home had risen in his lungs and coated his clammy flesh like sugar water. Her eyes, blue as the ocean and as deep as the center, housed a pool of darkness that had threatened to pull him under and eat him whole. They were a mirror of his own, a sinkhole so deep it drowned anyone who was ignorant enough to go for a swim.

'*I'll come back for you,*' Riam had screamed to her.

It had taken everything he'd had to force his feet to carry

him away from her. Leaving someone behind had cut him up, but it had to be done. Sacrifice the one for the many. That had summed up his entire godforsaken life.

It was a pipe dream, never leaving someone behind. The thought was a noble one, but not realistic in the least. People were left behind all the time, or so that was what he had told himself when he'd had to leave her. It was inevitable in times of war. *It's in the fine print.* It was the risk taken every time a soldier stepped onto the battlefield. They knew they could die on that field or be left to die alone. Every warrior alike knew those risks and took them willingly.

Movies gave people an unrealistic idea of what war was. It wasn't glamorous and no one came back the same. War was hell. War was wicked. It was a tar pit of pain and suffering. The reasons people were fighting never truly mattered, not to war anyway. War didn't care about good or evil. War couldn't give two fucks if there were wounded dying in the field or if an innocent was trapped under rubble. That's what war did — gave a man balls of steel then kicked them up into his throat with a bullet to the brain. The last thing he heard was the laughter of war. That was true war, not the shit they put up at the cinema, filled with romance and going home. No one went home, not completely. A piece was always left behind, a payment to war.

Riam had been front and center. He'd fought shoulder to shoulder with his people in endless wars against the evil and the wicked. And each time, he'd left people behind — good people, righteous people. They were his people, left in the trenches to save the innocents. Each time he stepped off the battlefield, war was beside him, clinging to him like a starved animal.

Riam — with no last name — was a Seer. That's what they were called. He didn't call himself that name any longer. He'd given that life up, willingly. He'd been a missionary, a hunter, a killer, a general in the Holy Wars. He'd been many things over his one thousand years — a lifetime of near misses and praying for his life to finally come to an end. But each day, he woke up. Each time he lay on his back, bleeding out, he woke up, having been dragged off the field. But he knew he'd live. He'd seen his own future in war, and it was a long fucking life. When death finally took him, he'd come back. His people always did, at least once.

Although he could see the future, he hadn't seen Sasha coming, the woman behind the door. He couldn't see her path. He knew because of his blindness toward her that her road was wicked — evolving and altering with each string she plucked — and that he would come face to face with her. She was like so many of his people that had changed the future. He had felt her manipulations in his bones the moment his eyes had locked with hers. It had left a taste on the back of his tongue — a sour flavor that told his brain to turn to go the other way. She was bad news.

Each time she'd changed the future to suit her needs, it had changed her own fate. A story that was once written for her now sat faded. She was a blank page to him, but he knew their paths would cross again. She could alter as much as she'd like, but destiny still had a way of working itself out, only more would die than originally planned. More would suffer and more pain would come. It was the way of his people. *When you fuck with fate, fate fucks you back.*

Riam and his people came from a long history of face palms and fate fucking. Sasha wasn't the first to alter the future, she had learned from the best. They'd paid dearly for trying to reweave the fabric of time not yet passed. They'd all had suffered for what they'd done, but it was nothing compared to what mankind would face.

The history of his people was warped. Riam's people were created to battle against the shadows. Their creator was none other than the Orygin. Banishing the darkness to Hades, the Heavens were created and man flourished. Riam's people were granted freedom to live among man. Some chose to remain behind. They were formed into Watchyrs, Healers and Messengers. They would become the light above.

Riam's line had walked among mankind. His direct descendants had come from the line of Laocoon. Laocoon, a Priest of Apollo, a Seer, had broken his vows to the gods by fathering two sons, Antiphantes and Thymbraeus. As punishment, two serpents were dispatched and attacked Laocoon and his sons. It was said that the eldest son Antiphantes had lived. He had fathered children with a Sibyl, an oracle, a Vampyre. They had birthed the future of hybrid Vampyres, Seers.

Like every other species walking the earth, there were varying stories of his origin. Riam didn't care where he came from—not anymore, not after one thousand years. All he knew was that when he died, he'd come back a hybrid Vampyre and live out his days until someone bigger and better than him took his last life.

He'd walked away from life as a Seer. He'd left behind the wars, the fighting and thinking the Seers had somehow done something great for humanity. They hadn't. The path they had interrupted by their acts had only created room for more hate and evil. Seers had been the difference between one person dying and one hundred, them causing the larger number. Their righteous wars had been nothing short of judgment day and murder. Riam had not been able to be who he was born to be. He'd lost the right to call himself noble and honorable. They all had.

On the floor of his bedroom at the Slayer compound, Riam felt the weight of his body lessen. After willing himself to calm, he searched for Sasha with his birthed abilities. Abilities he hadn't used since the day he'd walked away from his people were on the tip of his fingers. Opening up to this extent made him vulnerable to a bombardment of visions and voices. He'd learned how to shut down and control his Seer side. They were the same teachings he'd passed on to Desdemona, to help her control her Kler' abilities.

A person would grow mad, deranged, having to listen to the whispers of the wicked. The asylums were filled with Klers who couldn't control their abilities. They were a hairpin away from leveling the block or imploding. He, himself, was an inch from that insanity to find Sasha.

During the raid, he'd let the wicked parts of himself out, to uncover where Sasha was. He thought he'd be able to sleep just fine at night, letting out his own wickedness for a good enough reason, but he'd lied to himself. He had lied long enough to torture members of the Rancor Order. What he had done to those he caught alive was heinous and cruel.

He'd broken his word to his sister for the first time. He'd known it wouldn't be the last time he threw his honor to the side for Sasha. If she survived, he knew he'd be able to live with his decisions to reopen that chapter from long ago. If he found her alive, he'd be able to sleep at night — or so he hoped.

He had her name and a few details he didn't want to hear, but no location — at least, no location that was still standing. The men he'd questioned had paid — dearly, lengthily, for all they'd witnessed done to Sasha. But it hadn't been enough. No amount of abhorrent, beastly hate would be enough for the Order. Complete and utter annihilation wouldn't even touch the tip of what he wanted to do to them.

Sasha Grant. It was enough to send him on a hunt, digging up everything he could on her. It had taken a few days, but he'd found records of an explosion that had claimed the lives of two children and their father. Their mother had been spared, thrown through the front window. The photo in the paper was of Sasha sitting on the curb in front of her leveled home and burned life. She hadn't aged a day. The only change he'd noticed was in her eyes. Her eyes in the photo were bursting with tears and sadness. But now they were filled with vengeance, deepening the pool of wickedness looking back from under the lids.

A little more digging and Riam came up with a file from the Netherworld. The Rancor Order had been the prime suspects. They'd hit multiple locations — homes of officials and those who had alliances with the Netherworld — but this one didn't make sense. Sasha had no connections to the Netherworld, like the others always had. She'd been a full-time mother and her partner had been a public defender. They'd lived in the burbs—no social influences, nothing. But there had to be some connection. There always was. He just didn't know what it was yet.

Days previously, as Riam tossed and turned in bed, Sasha had come to him in a dream. One moment he was dreaming about a battlefield and the next he was staring down into the eyes of a fallen soldier, Sasha.

"Riam, help me," Sasha had whispered. Then she was gone and Riam was awake.

He allowed his mind to wander through the cobwebs of his abilities, then his body began to shake. His room was the perfect temperature, yet he was frozen to the bone. His marrow frosted and his blood slowed to a crawl, thickened from the arctic ice. Pushing his mind toward her, he saw nothing but darkness—like opening your eyes to find you have no sight. He followed the voice he'd heard in a dream.

"Sasha, I'm coming for you." Riam yelled out. A trickle of a whisper was all he could hear. The starved darkness ate up his voice.

Warning flares exploded in his brain. The darkness smelled like Strain…but more. On the back of his tongue, he could taste tears and fear and a bitter sadness. His brain screamed with the threat that he was in and sent his mind soaring back to into his body. Riam couldn't force his mind to stay in the void, even if he'd wanted to. Self-preservation always won out over curiosity.

Opening his eyes, he was on his back, staring at the wooden beams on the ceiling of his bedroom. He shut down his abilities, locking them behind the walls in his mind. He caught one sound on his way out, her muffled scream for help. It had been the faintest of whispers, but he knew he'd heard it. He felt every emotion in that scream, but what cut at his mind was the terror in her voice.

"Please," Riam whispered to himself, "someone help

her."

"Riam." Bane's voice came as a dull whisper, prickling at his ears.

Riam rolled his head to the side to find Bane on the edge of his circle, kneeling on the floor. Bane could step in, but Riam had taught him never to disturb a ring of protection. Bane's mouth was moving but his words didn't reach Riam inside the salt circle. Riam pushed his foot to the edge, his naked toe breaking the line of salt. His vision grew spotty, watching as Bane moved toward him. He was dimly aware of Bane pulling his shirt off then pulling his frozen body into the heat of Bane's beast. Bane naturally ran hotter than anyone else in the house. Then Bane's heat was blistering against his trembling, frostbitten flesh.

"Well done, young chap," Sid's voice whispered into Riam's mind.

Riam's head pulled back. Sid was standing at his side with a grin, cutting chunks off an apple and popping them into his smiling mouth. Sid shook his head, kneeling on the floor beside them, setting his apple down.

"This is gonna suck, big guy," Sid whispered again, with an unmoving mouth.

Riam gave him a nod and closed his eyes. "Sid, the darkness has her, The Genesys."

"I know," Sid answered out loud.

It didn't surprise Riam in the least. Sid seemed to know all things, much like he did, only Sid's ability to see was never affected by a person's path. He saw all. Sid never spoke out about his sight. Riam knew Sid couldn't. He knew it made Sid one of the most disliked people in the compound because of it. No one understood the burden that Sid carried. Sid knew when every single one of them would die and how, and he could do nothing. He knew the gory details of life, in all of its hateful glory, but he couldn't utter a word. The Orygin would kill Sid long before he could muster that word. Sid found ways around it, dropping clues here and there, but never enough to push it. You didn't fuck with the

Orygin.

Sid gave one last grin and reached out to Riam. The heat started at his toes and moved swiftly through his body. Sid grabbed Riam's arm and forced his body to heat from the inside. A blazing inferno melted the ice in his veins, like a frozen river breaking up and sending chunks of ice downstream. The chunks of ice smashed against his mind and body, ripping at him as they slid by. It felt like he'd endured hours of the blistering fire, yet only seconds had passed. To say it sucked was a gigantic understatement. He made a note to talk to Sid about his bedside honesty.

"You have company," Sid whispered, looking toward the bedroom door.

Riam took Sid's hand and slowly stood, internally bruised and confused. Who would be here for him? He had no one in his life that would come looking for him—no family and no friends outside this house—no one. Not even his people would come looking.

Bane let out a small growl, stepping in front of Sid and Riam. "Strain. It smells like Strain."

"Cute, little pup. You're protecting Riam and me? Of all the people in this house, Riam and I are the only ones who don't need protection." Sid chuckled, walking to the door. "It's not Strain. Guess again, hound dog."

Cael pushed open the bedroom door, poking his head in. "Riam, ah...someone dropped off an envelope for you. The messenger said you're expecting it?"

"I didn't give out our location," Riam said, frowning. He'd never given away the location of a safe house. Even under torture and the threat of death, he'd never once, during all of his wars, given intel.

"One of Bane's men—a shifter—showed up with an envelope. He said he doesn't remember how he got it. He woke up a few minutes from our compound with the envelope in his hand," Cael answered, moving to the side to let the three men out of the bedroom. "Something feels off, Riam. Des touched him to see how he got it and saw shadows and darkness. His mind is empty. A chunk is missing — like it had been carved out purposely."

Chapter Two

Leaning back in his black leather office chair, Deagon swiveled side to side, cleaning the fresh blow off the rim of his blistered red nostrils. He'd just done a snake-size bump off a hooker's ass. She was out cold on the floor, probably on the verge of another overdose. There was no better place for her than at his feet. She was one of the few who were still brave enough to step into his office and shut the door behind them. She knew what she was signing up for—a solid fuck and a few grams of coke. She was a regular around here. Not one of his working girls, though, he didn't employ trash. His girls were clean, inside and out. The tracked-up pasty lump on the floor was far from clean and would likely be his next reason for a dose of penicillin. *Good ole penicillin.* He popped those pills like Tic Tacs.

On his black lacquer desk sat a mountain of individually packaged grams of coke, ready to be picked up, but not before he sampled a few lines first. This one was better than the last baggie of crap he'd sucked down. The previous batch of California Cornflakes had been cut with enough laundry detergent that he could have opened his own Laundromat. Needless to say, his distributor's nose was bleeding just as much as his had the night before. Face meets curb. That was what happened when someone tried to make an extra buck or two from his supply.

Deagon had let go of his weak-assed persona 'Strain' six months ago, leaving him behind in the darkness of his father, the Genesys. At first, he'd felt lost, empty and no more important than the twitching whore on the floor. The burdensome duty of being Strain was gone, lifting the suffocating weight that had pushed him down dead-end roads off his shoulders. Slowly Deagon realized that it had been being Strain that had kept him in a state of foolish and rushed decisions, all to please a man that he truly didn't give a flying fuck about. It was the constant need to be more than who he was that had kept him pushing forward, into the darkness. Now, the soulless bastard he was, he would rebuild for himself and not that prick who had dumped him on the side of the street like road kill.

He was rebuilding, creating a new Order. He'd gotten the idea while watching a gangster flick on the net. He'd not only run the streets of Van City, he'd take out the Slayers, one pawn at a time. It was time to think outside the box, expand his little band of rejects to cover the country. Thinking big was where it was at. No more block by block, he would take the city and remove anyone who stood in his way. After he claimed it, he'd take another and another.

Leaning over his desk, the leather on his chair filling the silence of the room with a groan, he added to it with the whimper from his nose. With one long suck, he could almost feel the new holes form in his sinuses. This would either kill him or free his mind — both options he was fine with. Death would end the circus of his so-called life. He hoped for it but didn't have the balls to outright do it himself. He'd once thought of suicide as a cop-out. Now that he was faced with a shit-eating life, he couldn't man up and drag a blade across his neck or string himself up with a rope. Nope, living this life was the cop-out. Snorting his mind into freedom was an escape he desperately clung to. Plus, he had no idea where he would end up once dead. Back to Papa's darkness hadn't sounded like an end game he wanted a starring role in. Until he knew, he'd stick with the powdered-out-of-his-mind option.

Addiction was like breathing. It didn't seem important until it couldn't be done. There was no thought of it until it was cut off. He knew he needed help, but he had to go past his dealers on the way. He knew he shouldn't stop, but he pulled into the driveway anyway. There was no rhyme or reason to it, but it was stronger than any other instinct in his body. It was the only reason he woke up and breathed.

When he'd looked up addiction in the dictionary, he'd grinned. He knew it was uglier than anything ever written. It had said that addiction was an unusually great interest in something or a need to do or have something. Going by those terms, he was addicted to just about everything he liked – killing, fucking, drugs, booze, crime, fighting and breathing. Whoever had written the definition clearly had never struggled with the need to pump the body full of toxic waste. To him, addiction was more like playing Russian roulette. The one bullet would be the bad batch that finally took him out of the game.

As Strain, he hadn't been an addict. He hadn't been able to stand the shit. Now, as Deagon, having his link to power cut off, he'd needed the boost. It had started as a bump here and there. Then he'd become a full-blown coke-head, so naturally he'd started dealing. What better way to keep your personal supply at max than to be swimming in the shit?

Coke white was the new emo black around these parts. A person could drink their face off and walk home in a straight line, a few hundred bucks lighter. But honestly, who didn't have an addiction nowadays? *Pick your poison* – drugs, booze, social media, eating themselves into a double casket or fucking themselves into a fistful of antibiotics that didn't do a lick to stop the burning drip or keep them out of the cold earth.

He'd once had it all. Everything he had ever wanted, save those he wanted dead more than anything. He had apartments, warehouses and enough weapons to wage war against the neighboring country, money, cars, whores and power. It had gone hand in hand with a father that made Jeffrey Dahmer look like a Cub Scout leader. Now, he had an addiction and an itch burning his balls that he couldn't get rid of, with a mountain of debt he couldn't see over.

All or nothing rang truer now more than ever. He'd had it all and now he had nothing.

Soon. Slow and steady wins the race – or some inspirational shit like that. He cleaned off his mirror and tucked it in the right drawer of his desk. It was go-time, time to bring home the bacon. He transferred the product to a black duffle bag, dropping a few baggies of unlaced coke into his pocket before closing up his shipment of afternoon delights.

He'd spent six months improving the chemical additive. He had now perfected the compound. It no longer killed immediately, and it was virtually undetectable. His new product would be like every other gram of smack on the streets but cut with chemical shit that killed faster than the drug itself. Killing the irregulars then and there would be a heat-score he couldn't afford. He was now using the smallest trace amount, just enough to weaken the irregular. Over time, it would kill them, and he'd distribute his product throughout the country. His duffle bag was filled with the chemical-laced drug. He couldn't help but smile a bastard of a shit-eating grin.

Checking the monitors on the far cherrywood-paneled wall, he saw that his buyers were waiting at the table closest to the back, where all of his deals went down. Sure, he could call them into his office, but he wasn't that stupid. He did everything in public – less risk of shit going south. And in his experience, his life too often went south. He was exhibit A to that fact.

With a solid buzz going, he stepped out into his club. The music kicked him in the temples the moment his door opened. True to his word, he had gutted the place, starting from scratch. It was now a club with a one-month waiting list and a line around the block. The Hemlock was the place to be, which helped line his pockets.

His club manager Prudence, as usual, was waiting at his office door. He handed her the bag and stepped away. She followed behind him. She wasn't anyone's lackey – not anymore. She had risen from her knees in the bathroom to being the manager of The Hemlock — and a damn good one at that. With her behind the wheel, this place was making money hand over fist. The drugs were his deal, his cash, his addiction. The rest he left to her.

"Gentleman," Deagon said, taking a seat on one side of the small black table.

The two men in front of him didn't exchange pleasantries.

"Mr. Jackston." The bald one on the left — Mr. Nielsen — spoke with a small nod of acknowledgment.

No one went by first names and Deagon was sure Nielsen wasn't his true last name. No one cared about names. This wasn't about becoming BFFs — no Christmas cards exchanged and no campfire stories shared. This was business, pure and simple.

Nielsen leaned forward with a small white-cloth handkerchief. He motioned to Deagon's nose. "You appear to be bleeding."

Deagon brought his hand to his nose, pulling his fingers away tinged with blood. Taking the cloth hankie, he nodded. "Thank you, Mr. Nielsen." Then, "Prudence." The single word was all he would need to say.

Prudence, who was dressed in her usual black pantsuit and three-inch stilettos, placed the black duffle bag on the floor under the table, between Deagon and the buyers. The man to the right, Mr. I-Probably-Take-Horse-Steroids, slid a large envelope under the table for Prudence.

She tucked the manila envelope under her suit coat then stepped away. It would be counted, verified, then she would return with an approval. If she didn't give the all-clear, the buyers wouldn't be leaving upright. Deagon had enough men in this place to take out a bank. These two would be nothing more than a warm-up for the night. Part of him was itching for a no-holds-barred fist fight, but he needed the cash more than he needed to pound someone's face into a table.

Small talk wasn't something Deagon enjoyed, so he didn't bother. He didn't care how their lives were. He didn't care if they lived through the night. He didn't need his old abilities to know the two men across from him were irregulars. They tended to stand out like sore and arrogant thumbs. It bothered him in some odd way that he had to do business with those he hated. One day he wouldn't have to, but for now, he'd take what he could get.

Prudence returned with a nod. The men stood, extending their hands, shook, then took their shit to leave. They didn't bother checking the product. They were like Deagon. They'd be back if the shipment was light, and his shipments were never under.

"We need to talk, Deagon." Prudence spoke firmly, standing in front of him when he got up.

"Oh?" He said, rolling his eyes and sighing. He knew what was coming next.

She scoffed and rolled her eyes back at him. "Look at you. You're high as balls. You're snorting more and more of your own product – the shit you once hated. You wanna sell? Then sell. But this shit has to stop. You're damn near bleeding all over your buyers."

Deagon stood, smoothing his dress shirt and tie then putting the bloody rag in his pocket. "You're my club manager, not my mother. Don't overstep."

Prudence stood, hands on her hips, scowling. "And you're a pathetic addict, a real winner, Deagon."

Deagon reacted before his brain clicked into place and told him what he was about to do was stupid. He grabbed her arm and dug his angry fingertips in. She'd be bruised tomorrow.

She smiled. Of all the reactions to have, she smiled. "Are you going to hit me? Do it, Deagon. Be *that* man. Be the man you've hated. Be the man who hits women. Why not? You're already a drug addict. Why not add fucking loser to the list?"

Deagon let her go, staggering backward as if she'd struck him.

She followed him, leaning her body into his, whispering

into his ear. "If you touch me again, I'll kill you in your sleep. I don't need you to see me coming to get satisfaction from your death. Touch me in anger and I'll burn your fucking club to the ground with you inside. No man touches me without my permission. I'm *not* one of your fuckin' whores. I'm the only one who has stuck by your side. Why, you may be wondering? I'm starting to question that myself."

Prudence nudged his shoulder with hers as she walked away.

Deagon locked himself behind his office door, shaking. Part of him wanted to snap her cocky little throat. The other part couldn't do this on his own, not yet. He'd apologize, because he needed her — for the time being. Once he didn't? Well, that was a different story.

Taking a seat in his office chair, he felt his cock twitch. Her standing up to him had turned him on. One moment he wanted to rip her fucking head off and the next, he wanted to ram his cock down her arrogant little throat.

Looking to the floor, he saw the whore was stirring. He'd take what he could get right now, which seemed to be the story of his life. He pulled his fly open, releasing his cock, and knelt behind the woman whose name he couldn't remember. She didn't make a sound as he pushed inside of her. She woke and ground her hips against his but made no noise. When his release came, he pulled out and let himself go on her back. The release did little for him, except free the tension in his balls.

What a life. What a fucked-up life indeed. It would get better. Either he'd succeed or he'd die. He was good with either outcome. He pulled his pants closed, opened his planner and began detailing his next steps.

He would flood the market with tainted drugs. He would slowly rebuild the Rancor Order then go after Cael and Des. Once he took out the Slayers, his father — the Genesys — would come for him. He'd kill dear old Dad, one way or another. Then he'd have his victory. He sat with his eyes closed, leaning back in his chair, planning. Although he knew he had to do this slowly and deliberately, he needed a leg up. He needed connections.

Chapter Three

"It's from Myranda," Riam whispered, staring at the yellow manila envelope in his hand. The front of the envelope showed Riam's name and nothing more, but he knew the writing.

"Who's Myranda?" Cael asked, leaning over Riam's shoulder to catch a glimpse cf the envelope.

When Riam had stepped into the front meeting room, the house of Slayers had gathered around the young Therian. Bane had pushed through the group to speak to the member of his pack. Colin, a wolf, had been on a standard perimeter run around the edge of his territory when a young woman had approached him. He'd remembered his wolf rising to the surface in warning, only to be shoved back down like a fist in his throat.

To Riam's knowledge, only another Therian could force Colin to eat his wolf—an Alpha. But Bane couldn't smell anything aside from Colin. Colin hadn't remembered anything more than the bits he'd already said. In a blink he was standing in the backfield of the Slayer's compound, holding an envelope with Riam's name handwritten on the front. He'd contemplated turning around and booking it, but he'd known he had to see Riam. Something inside him had told him to find Riam. Whatever could scrub his memory like a Master Vampyre, make him swallow his animal like an Alpha Therian and control like nothing he'd seen before, had told him to run toward Riam and not away.

"It smells of Strain," Bane said pointing at the envelope with a growl following.

The Slayers hadn't heard from Strain in months, since the

Cleansing of Blood Alley. He was a ghost. They knew he was still alive. They'd found traces of him here and there. The Rancor Order was in the wind. Small raids conducted by the Order were still happening, but nothing nearly as significant as previous full-blown attacks. Proletaryans hadn't been seen since the Slayers swept up the mess during the raids, but they knew Strain was still alive and kicking. That's the thing about infestations. The vile creatures had to be exterminated — every last one of them — or they returned with their friends.

"Myranda was my Aegys," Riam whispered. He frowned, staring at the penmanship.

"Your Aegys?" Bane asked.

Riam nodded and looked up at those who had moved into the room with him. "From a time I do not wish to discuss."

"What would she want now?" Cael asked. "Fuck, do you have to leave us? Are you being called back to 'a time you do not wish to discuss'?"

Riam smiled and shook his head. "No, I would not be called back. My old life? It's gone and there is nothing to return to."

Cael grabbed at his chest, letting out a breath of relief. "Thank God. We can't lose you."

"Someone has probably perished, and she is reporting." Riam lied flat out. He did not speak with anyone from his old life, nor did they find a reason to communicate with him.

"Why the hell would it smell like Strain?" Bane asked, not giving up on the glaring fact that whoever had dropped this off wasn't Myranda.

Riam shrugged. "I don't know."

Bane gave Riam a hard look then let it go when he met Riam's gaze. Riam and Sid were the only members of the Slayers who could lie to a Therian without a change of pulse or smell. No one pushed Riam for more information. He said what he could and the rest couldn't be forced out of him. Riam didn't bend for anyone, come hell or high water.

He kept his secrets. After all of these years, no one pushed it with him. Sid, on the other hand, they hounded like there was no end.

Riam walked away from the front room to his bedroom. He shut the door and walked over his salt-covered floor, to take a seat on his goose-down bed. He closed his eyes and smelled the envelope. It smelled similar to the darkness that was holding on to Sasha. He breathed it in and let his mind wander, but he didn't go too far. There was nothing but a pitch-black void that waited to pull him in and no circle of salt to protect him.

Like dipping a toe in ice-cold water, he pulled back, shivering from what his mind had touched. He opened his eyes then pulled the envelope open. One white card sat inside. It looked like Myranda's writing, but something was missing. Myranda had never moved past old-school calligraphy. This writing looked too modern to be made by Myranda.

Sasha Grant is alive. Gretel's Emporium, midnight sharp.

Riam checked his watch. He had two hours to get there. Gretel's was in downtown Van City and had a reputation for being on the darker side of things. Her products catered to the dark arts and nothing in between. Riam knew of Gretel but had never had reason to meet her. What he did know about her, he didn't like. She dabbled in a world she didn't understand. He hadn't seen the need to ever venture into her little shop of horrors. It had nothing for him, and even if it did, the dark arts made his skin crawl. His stomach rolled when he was near someone who was a dark practitioner. Tonight he'd probably vomit on his shoes.

He didn't know who had dropped off the note, but whoever it was had known Sasha — or in the very least, of her. That was enough to push Riam to his feet. He dressed in full hunting gear, minus a few guns. He pulled on black leather pants, a leather jacket, strapped two knives on each

thigh and one gun in a holster under his jacket. Whoever—
or whatever—had written the note, he would be ready for
them. With or without the weapons, he could take down
almost anything that came his way. He knew he was just
that good. Hundreds of years of wars and brutality had
honed his skills. But just in case, he liked being prepared.

For the first time since stepping up beside Cael, he left
without telling his comrade a word. Going behind Cael's
back sliced at his soul. He'd always been upfront and
honest with Cael. But he knew if he were to have gone to
him, Riam would have been forced to bring half the Slayers
with him. He couldn't risk them, not when he didn't know
what the hell he was going up against. Deep down, this
betrayal was out of his love for his fellow Slayers and not
out of mistrust or because he was a traitor. He wouldn't
lead sheep to the wolves. He'd sooner walk into a trap and
die alone than watch his team die in his place.

It wasn't hard for him to sneak out without being noticed.
Riam could come and go like a breeze. He was made of
shadows when he needed to be. One moment he was just
there and the next, he was gone. They were the traits of a
warrior, traits he hated but deeply depended on. *Damned if
I do and damned if I don't.*

* * * *

With his stomach twisting into knots and his evening meal
threatening to end up on his black leather curb stompers,
Riam pulled open the door of Gretel's little shit shack.
Little bells on the door made his ears twitch. Glancing up,
he could see they were little brass bells, hanging to ward
off evil spirits and witches. He almost laughed, given that
the evilest thing in the shop was her. He wondered for a
moment if evil could ward against evil. He wasn't curious
enough to ask her if her shit actually worked. Her belief
in the craft was dangerous enough. He lumped her into
the same group as he put most right-wing zealots—group

Crazytown.

The smell, rolling on top of too-hot air, hit him in the face as soon as his boot touched carpet. Incense burning left a smell that he could taste on the back of his tongue, a failed attempt to cover up the smell of Hades. Nothing she could burn would ever remove the smell of sold souls.

The shop housed everything someone who wished for Hades to open up and swallow them whole could want. Glass shelves lined the walls of the store, with little bookshelves in the middle. It looked like every other shop on the block, only this one would peel your soul away from you like a gorilla with a banana.

Standing behind the far counter was the one and only Gretel. Her frizzy brown hair piled up on her round head bounced as she looked up from her book. Her gray eyes glittered, an empty soul looking out from behind them. Her smile made his skin crawl. It was as empty as a light bulb. Nothing about her was trustworthy. She'd need a soul for that, and she had nothing that even came close inside her shell of a human body.

"I've been expecting you, Riam," Gretel said, still smiling. Her voice sounded like she'd swallowed sandpaper or smoked two packs of cigs every day of her forsaken life.

Riam didn't want to step into the shop any farther than he already had. But as Gretel reached under the counter and lifted a small white box, he had no choice. She pushed it to the edge of her black countertop then waited for him. "This is for you."

Riam stepped forward to walk on into the shop. It felt like walking through cobwebs. The energy in the air was like sitting in a room filled with homicidal maniacs who were itching for another kill. It was negative, yet exciting. Everything about this place screamed evil. His soul bounced around inside his chest like a squirrel on crack, wanting to get out, readying itself to dig a tunnel and escape to a safer place. He wanted to get the hell away from the shop of lost hope.

Being up close and personal with what this place resembled, he almost didn't reach for the package. Knowing that whatever was in that box had come from the gift shop of hell had made him pause. Riam wasn't one to hesitate, but there was always a first time for everything. Now would be that time.

"Who left this here?" Riam asked, his voice cracking from nervousness.

"I wish I could tell you, but I simply don't remember."

Riam nodded. He was sure that whatever had happened to Colin had also happened to Gretel. Picking up the box, he turned his back on her. He wasn't about to stick around. There was nothing he could ask her bad enough for him to want to stay. Hell, she could have the recipe to the secret sauce and he'd still walk out. Whatever was in the box could be looked at outside. Another moment in this place and he was liable to vomit all over her pretty books and drying herbs from the garden of Hades.

There was a small part of his humanity that wanted to turn, grab her by the scruff of the neck and slap the stupid out of her, but he kept moving forward and his lack of genuine care kept his mouth shut. If she wanted to play with fire, so be it. Let it burn her little shop of ignorant bliss to the ground.

Letting the door slam shut behind him, he breathed in the cool night air. He cleansed his lungs with the smell of city life. His eyes burned from the incense in the shop. He knew it would stick to him like that putrid body spray teenage boys used.

Stepping into a side alley, he opened the little white box that smelled of Strain. He didn't think Strain himself was sending him presents. He'd have attacked Riam by now. Strain was too cocky not to jump Riam when he thought he had a chance. But the scent of the evil bastard clung to the white box as if it were made of his very flesh.

Inside the box sat a small black stone. The light from the lamppost glinted off the shiny stone. It was wrapped in a small wire and laced onto a thin leather string. He lifted it out of the box, staring at it. Under the flap that closed the box, a small note was inscribed.

You asked for help. This will help you hide from the darkness.

Riam frowned. He had asked for help, but more so, he'd asked for someone to save Sasha. Was he meant to be the one to save her? If so, who the hell was helping him? He knew it wasn't Strain. If Strain didn't already have her but found out where Sasha was, he'd have taken her for himself, again. He'd have tortured her and killed her already, sending pieces of her to the Slayers. Riam knew it wasn't the Genesys. The Genesys helped no one but himself. But someone was helping Riam. He just didn't know who or why. And he didn't know if he could trust that help.

He put the stone in his pocket. If someone was gunning for him, they'd have taken him out already. He'd use whatever help he could get right now. It was his only option.

"Well now, aren't you a crafty devil?" Bane said, stepping into the alley.

Riam sighed, looking to the opening between the buildings. He'd known Bane would find him. Every scenario of this moment he'd played over in his mind always included Bane. Bane had followed Riam around like a lost puppy, leaching off every drop of training he could. He knew that Bane respected him more than Riam respected himself. More than that, Bane would disregard a direct order to protect a member of the Slayers. That was Bane. He followed his moral compass more than orders.

"Are we going to talk about this, or are we just going to pretend that it has something to do with a bullshit future?" Bane asked, leaning against the wall beside Riam.

Riam didn't know what to say to Bane. If he told Bane what was going down, Bane — in all his loyalty — would fess up to Cael when asked. Bane, as great a Slayer as he was, was a shitty liar. When he tried, he had too many tells. He couldn't keep eye contact and he fidgeted during his lie. His pulse sped up and an oily sheen of sweat covered his upper lip. But if Riam said nothing, Bane would grow concerned and would go to the Slayers anyway. *Rock and a hard spot.*

Riam did the only thing he could do. He lied. "I'm not comfortable talking about my personal life, Bane."

Bane grinned and wiggled his eyebrows. "Are you telling me that you're banging Gretel? I mean, she's hot in her own way, but I thought you had higher standards than that."

Riam rolled his eyes. "No, I'm not *banging* the shop owner."

"Who is it then?"

"Who I bed and who I do not is not your business, little wolf."

Riam pushed off from the wall and beat pavement. Bane followed him out of the alley, still asking questions about who Riam was meeting and why. At first, Bane joked. But behind every joke there was truth and Bane's truth grabbed Riam by the throat.

Bane touched Riam's elbow, pulling at his attention. "All jokes aside, Riam. You and I both know you're bullshitting me about why you're down here. You don't want to come clean? Fine. You want to go behind Cael's back? That's your business. But when you need help, please call me. I'm always there and I'm solid."

Riam stopped trying to step away from Bane, turning his head to the wolf. "Thanks, Bane."

Bane nodded. "You weren't down here, and I didn't see you. I have a feeling this one is going to sucker-punch us in the throat, and I don't want any part of that headache. Word to the wise... Speak up before this problem speaks for you."

Riam knew Bane was right. He hated how right the little wolf was. But what could he do? Where did he start? He couldn't exactly tell his comrades that the reason they were Slayers was because of Riam and his people. He didn't want them to know who or what he was. He couldn't bear to see their faces when they found out he was a Seer — or the fact that someone who smelled like Strain was helping him find Sasha. That would go over like a lead fart. He was screwed, six ways from Sunday. They all were. And Riam was the cause of it all.

Chapter Four

Sasha didn't flinch at the darkness. It was an old friend of hers, a feeling that was familiar. After the light of her life had been extinguished, there was only room for the pitch blackness of her hate and anger. There was something comforting in the obscurity she was suspended inside of. She knew she should be terrified, but she wasn't. Inside this bubble of nothingness, there was gut-wrenching solitude and loneliness — she had grown accustomed to both.

Hanging in the dark like a piece of meat left to rot, it felt like years had passed. Forever had come and gone, leaving her behind. There were voices, murmurs whispered here and there. At first, she had gotten her hopes up. It was a defect of having a pesky soul. It had more hope than she'd wanted to have. Having a soul went hand-in-hand with having hopes and dreams. She had once loved that about herself, but now it was a bigger pain than floating around inside a chunk of shadow.

There was something peaceful about loneliness. There was strength in having nothing. When everything you had ever loved was taken from you and you had nothing to lose, there wasn't a thing that could be used against you. You feared nothing. The worst that could be done was death and at that point, death was welcomed by most of the lonely and destitute.

Hearing the tiniest of whispers, she wondered if someone out there was trying to rescue her. She decided it was more likely that there had been someone else strung up with her. Either way, she was content hanging in the shadows and waiting. For what, she didn't know yet. She'd be killed or she'd walk away. She was fine with either. One would end her pain and sadness and one would give her the chance to bring her vengeance to light.

"Say yes, Sasha." The voice whispered through the darkness.

The voice had come to her days or hours or weeks ago. Time had no meaning here. It could have been mere minutes or even years. She didn't know. It was the only clear voice she could hear. His voice was the only one that spoke directly to her and not faded like the murmurs she would catch here and there.

"Allow me to birth a child with you, and I will give you back what you have missed. Give me one child. I will remove the memory of that child and give you back your family," the voice said, calmly. The voice was almost soothing to her ears. Her soul was thirsty for contact.

Sasha grinned to herself. She knew that no matter what promises the voice gave her, she would never get back what she'd lost. Fate didn't bargain with anyone. It wouldn't give back what it had taken. She had tried that already, manipulating fate to give her the partner and children she'd always dreamed of and just look where that gotten her. They'd been killed in a house fire and she'd been saved — saved as a punishment for changing the course that her life, and theirs, should have gone.

"You doubt my abilities?" he asked.

"I'm very sure of your abilities, but I am surer of fate than I am of you. So no. The answer is no. I will never give you what you want," Sasha answered.

"Imagine waking up, your two children jumping on the bed, your partner's laughter filling the room as he comes in with your morning coffee. Imagine tucking them in, kissing their sweet foreheads."

Sasha squeezed her eyes closed. She couldn't feel the tears, but she knew they were rolling from the corners of her eyes. They always came the moment she thought about them. She didn't want to imagine her lost family. She didn't want to remember each time she was awoken by their laughter. She wanted to keep those memories locked away where they couldn't scratch at her soul. Each time they bubbled up, they left her feeling like she had been kicked in the heart. She protected those memories. They were the only reason she breathed. She feared if she thought too long on them, she would use them up and they would disappear.

She would be lying to herself if she didn't admit how absolutely wonderful it would be to wake up from this nightmare, to have her family back. Even for one minute, she'd have traded the world — just one last hug, one more kiss, a simple goodbye. But she knew that would never happen. She would never touch them or see them. No matter what the voice told her, that part of her life was gone.

"Say yes and I will take away the pain. Say yes and I will put you into a deep sleep and when you wake, you'll have no memory of your time with me. You'll have no memory of the past twenty-one years. You'll awake with your family, at home, and never will you be bothered by me or anyone of my line. You'll live out the rest of your existence, happy and loved. You'll watch your grandbabies grow and produce their own offspring. Say yes and I'll pay your debt to fate."

She rolled her head side to side. The debt was already paid. She knew his words and promises were as empty as the void where she was being held. "I won't do it."

"I'll give you my son, the man responsible for taking your future from you. I'll give you his people."

Her stomach twitched at the thought of wrapping her fingers around Strain's throat and squeezing out his life. She thought of every moment she had spent as his prisoner and every moment she'd wished she could kill him. She hated him for what he had done to her when he had her. But Strain's inner darkness was nothing compared to her own.

"You will say yes, eventually."

Sasha felt the cold touch of the darkness on her stomach.

She tried to scream, but her voice was eaten by the shadows that held her. The coolness spread through her body, filling her muscles and marrow. Her teeth chattered as her body began to vibrate with the frost forming on her soul. She wriggled in pain. It was a cold so great that it was burning a path through to her core.

"Say yes!" he screamed.

"Fuck you," Sasha tried to yell back, her voice came out as a whisper.

She'd let him kill her before she gave him what he wanted. She would never birth another child. She'd certainly not have something precious taken from her again—not in this lifetime or the next. Creating another personal hell was not something she'd willingly sign up for. Round two was not in the books for her.

She closed her eyes and wept. She cried for her failures and successes. Each success formed the biggest failure of her life. She mourned for her family and the fact that she was to blame for their deaths. She blamed Strain, but she was truly the only one responsible. She screamed until her throat couldn't make another sound, finally shutting down. Her soul whimpered from the emotional attack of memories.

Chapter Five

Deagon bought his way into the underground fight with a few bags of blow, laced with chemical. Midnight rolled in with him standing on the edge of a circle built of old tires. Inside the makeshift ring of rubber were two men — barely old enough to be called men — landing raw knuckles on each other in hopes of walking away with a few hundred bucks and a title no one gave two shits about.

Deagon could hear the bone-on-bone crunches over the screams for more blood and even death. Each blow came with a crowd calling for more. *Barbarians in their natural habitat,* Deagon thought with a chuckle. Dancing around the ring were half-dressed women, flaunting what their momma gave them. From what he could see, it appeared every man in this place had sunk his prick into them. Deagon couldn't imagine taking their sloppy seconds...and thirds. *You can take the girl out of the trailer park, but you can't take the trailer park out of the girl.*

Scanning the crowd that had packed into a warehouse basement on the edge of Van City, Deagon felt hopeful. The room was dank, moldy and probably had every disease known to man just waiting to invade with the first scratch of metal on flesh. This was the perfect scene for ground zero, the next pandemic. Deagon shivered with goose bumps. This place was a dump, but it was perfect for why he was there.

He was rebuilding his ranks on the backs of humanity — rejects kicked to the curb by mankind. The disadvantaged underdogs would become his lapdogs. Boys who grew up with next to nothing would be promised what the rest of the world took for granted. Food, a warm bed and safety in numbers, the very basics he knew they'd kill for. And in turn, they'd become his rebuild project for the Order. This time, built in his image.

For months, he had been attending these little bruised-up soirées. Every Friday and Saturday night, a fight to the bone-breaking end would be housed in an abandoned warehouse down Blood Alley. After each shindig, Deagon had left with three or four men, all willing to keep the fight alive. All Deagon had to promise was security and cash. Both were easy to supply. It was a more than fair trade, with Deagon getting a larger chunk of the pie.

Deagon straightened his suit and leaned against a stack of tires. The room smelled of gasoline, road tar, sweat and blood. Behind the stench, he could smell what he could only describe as determination. There was no room out there for quitters. Victory only went to the man who kept getting back up. He liked that about these fights. No one threw in the towel. Even beat down with swelled-shut eyes, they were always ready for more. And for what? A few bucks? Nope. It was because the slums of Van City didn't have room for the pathetic. Only the strong survived a life not even fit for a mangy dog.

He watched fight after fight without placing a bet or making small talk with the leeches that roamed the room looking for an easy mark. To his surprise, he turned down a round out back with some skank that looked like she knew what she was doing. It almost pained him to decline. She wasn't one of the trashy tire dancers. Deagon had seen her a few times at these events, earning a few bucks. He was higher than usual, which came with a snag. He could fuck or he could keep sucking down blow and fuck himself. Being this high, he didn't care. He probably couldn't get it up anyway.

His wandering mind was torn from thoughts of hookers and head by the sound of alarms. Like every fight, it came to a halt with warning of the imminent arrival of a storm of badges and sirens.

Deagon pushed off the tires and made his way to the four he had selected throughout the night. Not the winners. *Fuck the winners.* Winning proved nothing, apart from knowing how to land a solid blow. He wanted the ones who kept getting back up. He wanted the losers who were pissed off at the loss. He needed the ones who were leaving empty-handed and hungry for a win. He didn't have room for the winners and their plumped-up egos or those who thought they deserved respect. He sought men who would fight for every inch and earn that respect. *Fuck the rest.*

Slipping a business card into all four greedy hands, he walked away. There was a time and address listed on the card. They'd be there. They always came. They had one hour to make it to Deagon's new compound. It wasn't as glamorous as the last one had been, but it was a start and probably nicer than half of the rat traps they were going home to that night.

Deagon stepped out of the back door and into the shadows. The po-po charged in the front. Rarely did they come through the back, through the darkness. No one trusted the dark. He didn't blame them. The darkness ate at your sanity. But Deagon didn't fear the dark. Nothing in this world would come close to the darkness of his father. His father was what ate the night.

He wasn't used to the lack of power—not yet. He still felt like something was missing, a part of himself that had looked over his shoulder for him—a power that could send him warning signals whenever trouble was brewing. Now, he had to count on instinct that he hadn't quite honed. Hence, the rebuild of the Order. He'd need someone on his six, now that Strain wasn't there.

Making his way down Blood Alley to his familiar surroundings, Deagon watched the night unfold. The prostitutes were like cockroaches, bleeding out of the alleys faster than the clientele could arrive. They took up their posts and waited for the cash to roll in. It always did. Johns came from all over the city to bend over a whore who was an irregular. There was something less disgusting about dropping drawers with a freak. It had turned into a rite of passage for the boys in town. Every one of them had spent a night with a skin hustler from Blood Alley.

The dealers made their way down the strip, blinged out and trolling for their next victim, which wasn't difficult. This chunk of the city was brimming with victims and barely holding on to survivors. No one moved to this neck of the woods unless they were ready to die.

Deagon walked past his club, The Hemlock. The line was down the block again. Business was going great. The club had been well established long before he came along. He'd banked on it. He kept the club at full capacity every night. He needed the cash and the front. He'd used a few bucks from the club to purchase a warehouse under the name of the club — Hemlock Holdings.

The front of the metal warehouse looked like every other warehouse in town — run down and dirty. A bit of an eyesore, it was just what he'd been looking for. Anything more would have marked the place for a B and E or two. He didn't need the headache.

He checked his watch and grinned as he pulled open the front doors with a screech of the metal. Rusted and hesitant, the doors gave up and let him inside. He stepped around boxes and over chunks of old shelving. The smell of the building's history reminded him of a back alley — garbage, blood, old sex and burned needles. It smelled like lost souls and broken dreams.

In the main room stood twenty men, above held the other twenty, recruited a few weeks ago. The law called them adults, but most of them looked like puberty had recently kicked them in the balls. Each one was sporting their most recent defeat in the ring — black eyes and cut lips.

"I'm sure you're all wondering why I've asked you to attend tonight," Deagon asked, cutting to the chase. Small talk wasn't his thing. "I've selected you to build a new army in Van City."

They hung on to every word. They absorbed it like water to parched sand. No one questioned him. Deagon stood at the front of the rundown shit shack, with his arms tucked behind his back. His shoulders were straight and his voice commanded attention. It didn't get any better than this. He watched them eat up every syllable like starved animals.

"You answer to me. Follow my orders or die. Once in, there is no way out. Toe tagged or left in a ditch, is your only escape. You have twenty-four hours to decide," Deagon said then stepped to the side, arm extended to show them the door. No one moved. No one walked out and no one needed a second to decide. They were in. They were his.

Deagon smiled, letting out a slow breath. "Very well. First, this place requires a facelift and a cleaning. You may remain here if you need. There are showers and also food, bedding and clothing on the second floor. I will be back tomorrow. We will begin training at once. Any of you who talk are dead. This is the only warning."

Deagon pointed at one man, Killian—an irregular, a Therian. He motioned Killian to step forward.

"Yes, sir?" Killian replied.

Killian stood at six feet tall, built solid. His long brown hair touched his shoulders in waves. He stared forward, his attention fully on Deagon.

"Tell me, Killian. Why did you lose your last fight?" Deagon asked. "You're a werewolf. You could have ripped the man in half."

Killian gave a nod. "I didn't need to win the fight to win the war, sir. I only needed to injure him badly enough for him to need medical attention. Then, I could hunt him alone."

"That's not very fair," Deagon said, grinning.

"If he wanted fair, he shouldn't have come to Blood Alley. He should have stayed in his little sliver of privilege and caviar."

"Did you find him?"

Killian nodded. "Yes."

"Why did you want him dead?"

Killian smiled. "You don't touch my family. You can do what you want to me, but if you touch my family, I'll hunt you down and peel the flesh from your bones, slowly and painfully. He touched them."

Deagon's smile widened. "I'm happy to hear you put so much stock in those ties. Consider us part of your family."

Part of Deagon wanted to hunt down his family, just to test Killian, but he couldn't risk losing his men—not yet anyway. He was rebuilding and needed every able body at his disposal. Poking the wolf would have to come later.

"You're my new Calyph, Killian," Deagon said and shook his hand.

Deagon's chest burned and he stepped back. He was either about to overdose or have a heart attack. It felt like the mother of all heartburn, only his stomach was twisting into one large knot. Deagon went outside then pushed the palm of his hand into his chest, trying to calm his pounding heart.

He felt like a thousand eyes were staring at him in the darkness. Taking in a few deep breaths, he could smell the darkness, feel it pressing against his face. But it was different. It smelled like his father. He frowned when the pain in his chest slowly dissipated.

Deagon left his new band of social rejects to head back to his club. His money was on the fact that he was coming down off his perpetual high. He needed another hit before reality sunk back in and his heart finally gave out. He had many flashbacks of the time he had spent inside his father. Each time he came down, he was locked in that memory until he rebooted on a fresh batch of blow.

The Genesys stepped out of the shadows and watched his once pride and joy walk away from his new compound. He was now calling himself Deagon, but his son would always be Strain to him. He had been a few inches from Strain's throat and had watched Strain struggle with the power rolling over his flesh. Strain gripped at his heart as his father teetered on willing it to burst or keeping it pumping.

The Genesys took a final look at the new warehouse belonging to his son and fhaded back into the shadows. Even with his powers gone, his son had done as any Strain of worth would do—rebuild. This was a test, to see how resilient his bastard son could be. Like any lesson worth learning, this one would be learned the hardest of ways—on his knees and fighting tooth and nail. He wanted to see if his son could do it on his own and how much he'd gain by doing so.

The Genesys had a backup plan. He had to get Sasha to agree, and if he couldn't, he'd have to mend those fences with a son he hated. How would Strain take over the family business if he didn't learn control? The Genesys hated the idea of putting all hopes in a shell of a man he'd once called son. The idea turned his stomach. Strain would be the death of them all unless he could learn how to be a leader. The Genesys wouldn't bank on his son, but he was hopeful.

Chapter Six

"I don't fucking care what you were doing, Riam. You don't take off alone. We can't afford to lose you." Cael's scream bounced off the walls. It felt like Riam was being slapped repeatedly, with each echo of Cael's voice.

Cael pressed his white knuckles into the meeting room table. He'd beat his fists on the wood until it creaked in retaliation. At first, he'd paced. Each time he'd stopped to gather his thoughts into words, he'd shake his head and continue his walk.

Riam and Bane had gotten back to the compound an hour ago, and it had taken all of ten seconds for Cael to grab Riam by the shoulders to push him into the wall. His anger had been hot enough to feel it lick up Riam's cheeks like a wet crop. Cael had every right to be angry, and Riam took it because he deserved it. He took it because he respected the hell out of Cael. Although he had gone behind the Vampyre's back and was eating shit because of it, there was no other man he valued more than Cael.

When it looked like Cael was about to pop a vein in his neck, Riam and Bane said nothing. Neither of them were dumb enough to argue or excuse their behavior. Riam was sure Cael would have torn out a throat or two if either of them had muttered a single word. Controlling his temper was not a strong suit for Cael. Riam had kept his head down and Bane kept his mouth shut. Bane had stood his ground. Each time he was questioned, he'd say he hadn't known. Riam could tell that Cael knew the little wolf was full of shit but didn't push him.

"Never again, Riam. Do you hear me? You're not a fuckin'

one-man show. We go out in two-man crews. Go it?" Cael asked, pounding his fists on the table again. "I asked you if you fuckin' got it, Riam."

Riam nodded. "Yes, I've got it."

Cael looked to Bane and pointed his finger, glaring. "And you... Pull your fucking head out of your ass. You're part of a team, not Riam's team, *our* team. You're either with us all or not at all. Got it?"

Bane's eyes widened. "Yes, sir, I've got it."

Cael pounded his feet as he stormed from the room, mumbling to himself about having to babysit children.

Bane glared at Riam. "Asshole."

Riam didn't bother responding to Bane. Bane was right. Riam was an asshole. He was feeling it from all sides right now. Would it stop him from continuing down the path he was on? Not a chance. Shaking the night off, he stepped away from the table. Walking to his bedroom, he could hear Cael still mumbling down the hall, ranting at Des about his Slayers being small children who required a leash and a wolf who was too tight-lipped and covering for Riam. Riam had to give the wolf props. He didn't cave or squeal. He played dumb. *When in doubt, go with ignorance.*

"Aren't you just a basket of surprises, Riam? Mr. By-the-Book is shitting all over the rules he helped put in place. It's ironic...or would that be coincidental?" Sid said, stepping out from behind Riam's bedroom door. "Thanks to social media, I have no idea which one means what."

Riam shut his door and groaned. "Don't you have somewhere to be, Watchyr?"

"Nope, I'm all yours." Sid grinned. "Haven't you heard? I was fired, years back."

"Go be a pain in the ass to someone else, Sid. I'm not in the mood." Riam tossed his jacket onto the bed and waited for Sid to take his exit.

Sid shook his head, giving Riam a wink. "I thought you'd be interested in a new club down Blood Alley called The Hemlock. You look like you could use a drink."

"Unlike you, Sid, crawling into a bottle isn't going to solve my problems."

Sid pulled open the door. "A drink or two wouldn't hurt them either, Riam. Go. Check it out. First drink is on me."

Sid tossed a ten spot on the floor then left Riam to his thoughts. With the door clicking shut, Riam picked up the ten-dollar bill. He sat on the edge of the bed, thinking of Sid. Sid never came to Riam, never spoke to Riam about his woes or offered to buy him a drink. Sid was bordering on severe alcoholism and ridiculousness but never therapy.

Riam grabbed his jacket and headed out. He called out to Bane, "I'm hitting the bar. You coming with?"

Cael poked his head around the wall from the hall, giving Riam a long stare. "Where are you going?"

Riam shook his head. "The bar. You in?"

Bane jogged passed Cael in the hall and came into the front room, pulling on his shit kickers, bouncing from one foot to the next. He was still in full leather, always ready to roll. "I'm in."

Cael gave them both another hard look. He called for Sid to tag along with Riam and Bane.

Sid shuffled his way into the room. "Where are you two off to?" he asked, looking innocent.

"The Hemlock, a new club," Riam answered.

Sid shrugged. "I haven't heard of it, but I'm always down for a drinkie-pooh," he said, still concealing his role in the activities.

Riam shook his head then followed the two men out the front door. Bane and Sid bantered back and forth until they hit Blood Alley. Bane was one of the few who could take the shit Sid dished out, laughing and sending the insults back over. Sid tried low blows about Bane's mother, but Bane took it like a champ.

After finding a parking spot, Sid clapped Bane on the shoulder, keeping Bane from moving down the sidewalk. "This is as far as we go, little pup."

Bane looked from Sid to Riam and snarled. "Fuck me.

This shit is getting old, Riam. What the fuck do I tell Cael when he asks?"

"Tell him the truth, minus a few details. Let's go get boozed up. You'll be too drunk to talk about it or even remember the night," Sid answered.

Bane growled, glaring at Riam. "Do you know how much booze it'll take to get a Therian drunk? This is going to fucking cost you, big time."

Riam tossed Bane his wallet.

"You have one hour, my friend. Only one hour to understand," Sid called out to Riam. He turned to Bane with a smile. Nothing good ever came from that kind of smile. "Let Uncle Sid take you to your first strip club."

"Bitch, please, I've been to strip clubs." Bane laughed.

"Not this kind. Vixen is run by a Succubus. She's the only pure demon kicking around up here. She found a loophole in the rules and has been running Vixen ever since. As long as she stays in the club, no one cares."

"A demon? Are you fuckin' serious? Because we don't have enough problems already, you want to go messin' with a demon?"

Riam could hear them laughing back and forth as they walked away, arguing over risking their souls. But Sid assured the wolf that one night in Vixen's would be worth it. Riam set the timer on his watch. In one hour, shit would go down. Sid had given him a heads up twice now. He gave him the club, for a reason that he still didn't know. He gave him an hour, which he'd come to understand the reason for in an hour.

The sidewalk leading up to The Hemlock had a line down two blocks with ready-to-go partiers. Men and women smelling of sex, booze and drugs filled the chunk of concrete. They were nattering on about how dope the club was and where to score primo snow. Half were barely dressed and the other half were dressed in less than a napkin. Hairspray and sweat were thick in the air. Each breath Riam took in coated his lungs in chemicals.

Crossing the street, he took post beside a blue Dumpster and waited for the reason for going to Blood Alley. He hadn't been down to the heart of this area since the Cleansing. The locals had cleaned up the area, removed the chunks of the old city that the Slayers had taken to the ground. Buildings that had fallen were either empty lots or had been cleared and rebuilt. That was the thing about Van City. Every square inch of retail space was cleaned and set up, almost overnight.

Riam scanned the line. He watched those going in and out of the club—the staff and the passersby. The only thing he noted was his surprise at the volume of drugs that were pumping down these parts without more dead on the ground. He watched runners handing off baggies to the desperate. It was like watching mosquitoes on the old swamplands. Like flies to honey, the souls were stacking up, ready to fill their bodies with sin.

There was a part of him that was still angry that his entire youth had been stolen from him. He'd never known what it was like to be a kid or teenager or even an adult without worry. He had been born and aged to what humans would call thirty years old, then he'd stopped aging altogether. The mixture of his line kept him youthful on the outside, but he was old as fuck on the inside. He'd lived dozens of lives but had never been allowed to live the life he'd wanted—being normal, not having to kill. Having a sliver of sanity would have been just fine with Riam. Hell, just one day where he could throw caution to the wind and have a night of craziness… But no, he was always *on*, ready to wage war at the drop of a dime.

He watched as two young men in line, in their very early twenties, joked back and forth, both smiling, dressed to impress. Their biggest worry was who would get their rocks off that night. Two women wiggled their way up the block and pressed themselves into the two walking hard-ons. Riam watched as they interacted, softly and lovingly. All four were in their own little bubble, where the world couldn't hurt them. Part of Riam wanted to tap them on the shoulder and tell them that shit only went downhill from here. But deep down, he wondered what it would be like, to be that consumed with love.

Riam had never been in love, not truly. He had loved his siblings, he'd loved his comrades, but never once had he loved a partner to the point of almost pain. He'd watched his fellow Slayers keel over in agony of the heart from a love they felt. He'd seen it play out for those around him for hundreds of years, but never for him.

Did he have room in his life for love? Could he afford the risk? This wasn't a life he'd feel honored to provide a mate. They were always running and hiding and worrying about waking up the next day. And what if she wanted children? Riam had sworn never to produce offspring. He didn't want to give his children the burden of being a Seer. How could he wish those abilities on a child? But how could he tell his mate that he was taking away her chance to have a child, through his own refusal?

The alarm on his wristwatch sounded. A *beep-beep* told him that his time was up. He cleared away his pipe dreams and bullshit thoughts of one day being in love and truly happy then took a firm grip on his reality. That life simply wasn't in his cards — too many lines crossed, too many lives taken. He was pretty sure the Orygin wouldn't bless a man like Riam with a life worth dying for. The wicked were not rewarded. He — in all of his loneliness — was a walking example of the punishment handed out to those who fucked with fate.

Pushing off from the Dumpster, his heart skipped a beat when he saw what he know knew he'd been waiting for. Strain — in the fucking flesh — stepped out of The Hemlock — head to toe with an oily sheen that screamed 'addict', in two thousand bucks worth of top-shelf suit. Every fiber in Riam's body wanted to beat pavement and wrap his fingers around that little bastard's throat, not only for what Riam knew he'd done to Des and Neri and every other female he had taken but because he knew that Strain had to die.

"You have one hour." Riam could almost hear Sid whispering in his ear.

His hour was up. He'd been given just enough time to see what Strain was up to, but not enough time to get himself killed.

Between breaths, he could hear Strain talking to a drug lackey. The coked-out punk was talking about a new shipment coming in. The flunky was calling Strain by his old name, Deagon. Had Strain walked away from the Genesys? Likely not willingly. Riam was hopeful but not stupid.

Maybe he could talk to Strain, convince him—in his own special way—to give up the location of the Genesys. He took one step forward and went for another when a hand gripped his shoulder.

"Don't do it, Riam. You'd have more luck making a deal with a devil," a female's voice whispered in his right ear.

He breathed in her scent. "Strain."

Chapter Seven

The time had come for Bellum to step out of the shadows and into the light. Too many had fallen, more souls left in the dust to wither alone, for her to remain in the background. Her exile, inflicted by her father, the Genesys, was a punishment for going toe to toe with him. He was, after all, her creator. She had never been meant to rise up to become that powerful or that cocky.

Bellum had been grown in the womb of a Seer who had been promised to be cured of her blood disease. Her father had made good on his offer. He'd removed the disease, along with all of her blood, with a knife in her throat that left her on her deathbed. The Seer — Bellum's mother — was sent to Elysium, cured, in a way. Bellum would sooner make a deal with Ruynous than with her double-dealing father.

Bellum had been sent into the world by her father, as penance for her actions, with her memories taken from her. But during her rise to power, she had grown just as crafty as him. Before going against him to end his existence, Bellum had marked her entire body with wards against evil. Tattoos covered her flesh. It would be her only protection against a man who would drown babies for intel and kill families because he could.

When it had come time to land the killing blow, she'd hesitated. That hesitation had almost ended her life. Some would say that she had been given mercy, being allowed to live, but Bellum didn't see it that way. Her father's intention had been to send her out into the world without abilities or memory. That wasn't a kindness. It would have led to her death without her father having to take the blame.

For centuries, Bellum had waited. She'd waited for strength in numbers, for someone to step forward to fight with her, and now was that time. She'd heard Riam call out for help, in her father's darkness. Bellum would forever be linked to that darkness, but her wards protected her from her father's prying eyes. Bellum knew it was time. She could feel it in her bones. There were others out there, willing to die in order to bring her father down.

She'd sent word with a wolf to guide Riam to the shop. She'd had one stone left, a stone crafted from the original darkness. She'd given this stone to Riam. It would help him get Sasha back from the shadow that was her father. Bellum wouldn't allow another child to be born. She would give Riam the chance to rescue Sasha before she would need to be killed. Bellum didn't want to kill a Seer, but she would to protect humanity. She would bring this city to its knees if she had to. She knew deep down that she would do worse for the fate of mankind. There would never be another Strain, not while she still breathed.

Following Riam, she'd thought for sure that he would go to his comrades and tell them about the stone, tell them he thought he was being helped by a Strain, but he'd said nothing. He was going to try to save Sasha on his own. It hadn't surprised her. Seers weren't the type to drag others into harm's way. But what had really thrown her for a loop was the Watchyr, sending Riam to The Hemlock. Bellum didn't understand why Sidriel would lead a lamb to the slaughter.

She had watched Riam from the shadows, watched him lean against a Dumpster across from the club. The moment Strain had stepped out, her stomach flopped. As Riam took one step forward, so did she. The moment she touched Riam's shoulder, the shadows fell away and she was exposed. She knew what Riam would do. He would attempt to talk sense into a man who was too high to have common sense. It would fail, and Riam would bargain.

That bargain would cost too greatly.

"Don't do it, Riam. You'd have more luck making a deal with a devil," Bellum whispered into Riam's right ear.

Riam took a deep breath. "Strain."

It was as if she had all the time in the world. Everything slowed for her. She felt his shoulder bunch under her grip. She knew he would be turning to his left, pivoting around to face her. She felt her own heart speed up and her legs tense, preparing for an assault.

She didn't wait for the fight or for him to turn. She lifted her left hand and touched his temple, sending him every bit of knowledge of Strain, her brother. Through her eyes, Riam would see who Strain was and what he was capable of. Bellum had watched him for years, since the first time she'd felt his pulse in the back of her throat. She gave Riam the reality of Strain, the harsh coldness of who he was deep down. He was a Strain, but more than that, he was Deagon—pure evil. The Slayers may believe that her father was the one they needed to fear more, but the truth was, it was Deagon.

Deagon would bring the world to their knees. There would never be balance with him. There would never be peace. Deagon was who they had to take out, for he would be the end of all mankind.

Bellum removed her hand from Riam's temple then stepped back, pulling him deeper into the alley so he wouldn't be seen. What she had done to his mind was equivalent to using a hot poker as a Q-tip. He'd be a little disorientated, but not for long. Riam's mind was powerful and would bounce back within minutes. The only reason she was able to bring him down was due to him not using his own abilities. His mind had grown a little rusty when it came to sharing memories.

"Was that really necessary?" Sid asked from behind Bellum. "His ego is going to be all bruised up, and I'm going to have to listen to him bitch and whine."

Bellum dropped Riam on the pavement then turned to

face the Watchyr. She shrugged and smiled. "What was I supposed to do? Let him cross the street? He had to know, Sid."

"This shit ain't gonna fly with the Slayers, little war. They're going to hunt for you if you don't give it a fuckin' rest already." Sid referred to her with the nickname he always had since the moment he'd realized her name meant 'war'.

"I need their help to take out my brother and father. I'm tired of waiting, Sid," Bellum replied.

Sid nodded and waved her off. "He's coming to. Scram."

Bellum sunk back into the shadow of the brick wall, pulling the darkness around her. Many years ago she'd met Sid while he was driving a knife into her heart. She'd tried to take out Desdemona, the half-breed abomination, like her father. Each time she'd gone for Des, Sid had been there and would nail her to the wall. They'd struck a deal. If Des stayed on a righteous path, Bellum would help Sid keep the half-breed alive. If she faltered, Sid would take her out himself. It was as good as it got.

When Bellum decided it was time to come out of the closet in order to take down her father, Sid was there, questioning her. She knew he was only protecting Des, but Sid had become more like a rash than anything else. But if she hadn't told him the plan, there would be no plan. Sid would have let the Slayers know. Even if he hadn't come right out and said the words, they'd have known she was coming. Hell, Sid would have spoken the words then died to keep Des out of harm's way.

She watched Sid crouch down and slap Riam across the face.

"Rise and shine, asshole. You don't get paid to sleep on the job."

Riam pulled his eyes open and slapped Sid back. "I don't get paid, *asshole*."

Sid helped Riam off of the ground, brushing the dirt and garbage from his legs. "What the fuck happened, Riam?"

Riam glared, looking up and down the alley. "As if you don't know, Sid. Let's get the fuck out of here. I need a drink."

"Bane is still at Vixen's. I'm pretty sure he didn't even notice me leaving."

"How does the magick at Vixen's not affect you?" Riam asked.

Riam and Sid walked passed Bellum without pause.

"You can't use magick on magick. It's like trying to make water wetter or black blacker. I'm not human. I'm not alive but I'm not dead. I'm not really walking beside you, but here I am."

When they disappeared around the corner, Bellum followed them, careful not to bump into anyone or touch anything. She would follow them as she had time and time before. She had become their shadows, hoping they were the army she had prayed for all of these years in exile.

Chapter Eight

The trio left Vixen's after a few shooters, drinks, lap dances and a partridge in a pear tree. Getting Bane out of the club was like peeling chrome off a tailpipe. He had to stop to profess his undying love for every dancer and the bouncer before being dragged out. Sid and Riam packed the falling-down Therian home, as he swore on his mother that he was going back with a ring for the redhead in the back.

Bane dropped his head to the side and smiled. "I got your back, Riam. We were all at the club together, all night. I'm solid. I'd lie for you. I'd die for you, my friend. I love you."

Riam grinned. *That's a drunk male for you – all about the love.* "I love you too, wolf."

"I'm not an island. I'm more than my wolf," Bane slurred. "But I do like to howl and chase rabbits. It's so cool, guys. It hurts like a bitch to shift, but it's rad as fuck. I have these gigantic claws and teeth…" Bane trailed off, mumbling and slurring about random animals he'd eaten and times he'd shifted when he shouldn't have. He told a long story about a pair of shoes he'd just purchased then shifted in, ruining them. He told it in such a tragic way that Riam almost mourned those shoes with him.

In the front door of the compound, Sid tossed Riam back his wallet. "So you know, I wasn't the one who pissed through four grand in under an hour."

Riam watched Sid lift Bane over his shoulder and pack him through the house with a trail of vomit following behind and screams of his being forced to leave his love at the club.

"Fun night?" Cael asked, walking into the front room, staring at the floor in disgust. "Bane's, I presume?"

Riam smiled, nodding. "Vixen's club. Apparently it takes four Gs to get a Therian loaded. Tomorrow he's going back for some redhead in the back."

"Redhead? Since when does the Succubus employ redheads?" Cael asked.

"She doesn't. She thinks they're soulless and doesn't want the competition. I think Bane is talking about the guard dog." Riam laughed, shaking his head.

Before Riam could move away, Cael asked to speak to him, privately. Riam didn't want to do it but knew he had to.

"What's up, boss?" Riam asked, taking a seat in Cael's office. The metal chair touching his ass had seen better days. The chair moaned under the pressure of his two-hundred-and-forty pound, five-foot-eleven, all-muscled frame.

Cael poured himself a vodka on the rocks, sliding one across the desk for Riam as well. Cael took a seat and a pull from his glass. The noise of the ice cubes made Riam uncomfortable. Silence was never a good thing with Cael. It meant he was trying to come up with the right words. Needing to think about how to phrase something was always a bad sign.

"We've been through a lot, you and me, no?" Cael asked.

Riam nodded, taking a sip of his vodka. Cael only drank top shelf V. Smooth and it went down like water. "Indeed, we have."

"I wanted you to know. I'm here, Riam. I don't know what's going on, but I have an idea. I need to know if you're solid or if you need some time off."

"Time off? Are you benching me, Cael?" Riam asked, frowning and readying himself for an argument.

"Nope. You're the only one who can do that, Riam." Cael leaned forward, looking Riam in the eyes. It wasn't often anyone looked Riam dead in the eyes without squirming. "Having said that, I can't let you risk us all. That little wolf out there lied to my fucking face for you. He lied to his commander, for *you*. Shit like that doesn't fly here and you know it. Bane would die for you, Riam, just as everyone else here would. Yet you disrespect us and everything we stand for. For what?"

Riam sighed, letting out a chestful of air he didn't know he was holding. He did the only thing he could. He told Cael the truth. He started with the first letter and his belief that it wasn't from Myranda, but he hadn't told Cael before because he hadn't wanted to risk anyone in the house. He showed Cael the stone then told him what had happened at The Hemlock, along with waking up on the ground with memories of Strain that he hadn't had.

Cael nodded and stopped pouring drinks, grabbing for the entire bottle instead. With a white-knuckled grip on the bottle of sanity, he breathed deeply. He looked like he was trying to will himself to calm down.

"I'm working on my anger management issues with Des," Cael said, smiling through a clenched jaw. "*I feel* like I'm not worthy of trust when I'm fuckin' lied to. *I feel* like ripping someone's head off and shitting down their dishonest throats when that particular person goes behind my fuckin' back and risks us all because they're complete idiots."

Riam grinned. "*I feel* statements shouldn't involve violence or swearing, Cael."

Cael groaned then let out a shaking breath. "Thank you, but you've used up your turn to talk. Now it's my turn."

"Continue. Sorry for interrupting," Riam said, trying to keep the laughter from his voice. Riam knew Des was working with Cael on his anger. Every now and again she would pull him to the side to remind him to communicate and not just rant and rave. So far, it wasn't really working.

"Fuck it. Riam, what the *fuck* were you thinking? Why wouldn't you come to me?" Cael asked. "After all of these years, you still play your cards close to your chest."

"I don't know, Cael. There you have it. I don't fucking

know. I was scared. I didn't want anything to happen to any of you."

"And how the hell would we feel if you went out alone and got yourself killed?"

"Honestly, probably pretty fuckin' scared. Could you see me as a full hybrid Vampyre?"

Cael shot Riam a dirty look. "Yuck it up, asshole. That's not what I meant. You have two choices. Either you're all in or you're all out. I'm not fucking around, Riam. In or out. No more in-between. You want to keep your cards plastered to your chest? Fine. But no more bachelor-style outings. And Bane doesn't count. He has his snout so far up your ass that I can't tell which one of you is the wolf is anymore."

"I'm in, all in."

"Give me your word of honor that you will never pull this shit again," Cael demanded.

Riam lowered his head, shaking it. "I can't, Cael. My word is shit."

Riam remembered his sister, Layla. He'd given his word to her then broken it, hunting for Sasha. His word meant nothing. At first, he thought the booze was getting to him. His vision grew blurry and he felt like vomiting, until he realized his eyes were filled with tears and his shoulders were shaking so badly that it was stirring the booze in his belly.

"Fuck, Riam," Cael said, moving around the desk. "I didn't mean to be so hard on you. Shit, sorry. I'm sorry. I trust you. I trust you with my life. I was angry, I should have stuck to my '*I feel*' statements. It's okay, my friend. You're in. You're all in. I've got your back. Anyone who has a word to say about this can come and talk to me."

Riam lifted his eyes to Cael and did what he'd never done before. He got up, then hugged him. Riam knew Cael was surprised. His body had been tense, as though he'd braced himself for a blowout with Riam. Finally realizing that Riam wasn't about to go all knuckles on him, Cael held him in return. The bond of their friendship felt like a life raft to Riam, pulling him up and out of his deep pool of sadness.

"It's not that, Cael. I deserved every drop of your attitude. I can't give my word because it's already broken," Riam whispered. He told Cael the story about his sister's last dying wishes—for Riam to leave the hate behind, for him to live an honorable life. "I have tried, Cael. I have tried to be the man my sister would be proud of. I have tried to be an honorable Slayer, to live a life free of sin and war. I've failed Layla."

"No, Riam. What you're doing now to save Sasha is honorable. It's how you're going about it that's wrong. Layla would see you fighting to save a soul, and she would be proud of you. But you must do it the right way, or what the hell are we fighting for?" Cael asked, gripping Riam's shoulders. "You can do this, Riam. We will help you. We'll get Sasha back, together. You would never allow me to charge into Hades for Des alone. You'd be at my side, fighting tooth and nail with me."

"It's not the same, Cael. Sasha is not my Fyrvor," Riam pointed out.

Cael grinned. "That may or may not be true, but it is the same. It doesn't matter who we are going after. It is the fact that you would never have me face something alone. You would never step aside and let me risk my life, not without you."

Riam nodded. It took him a few tries to get the words out, but he thanked Cael. "You've always managed to bring me back from my darkness. Thank you. I need help, Cael. Sasha needs help."

Cael gave Riam a pat on the back. "You have it, always. Let me figure a few things out then we tackle this tomorrow. Now, go clean up your wolf's vomit before Des makes me do it. And I'm so not fucking cleaning that shit up."

A small knock brought their attention to the office door. Amity poked her head in. "I'm very sorry to interrupt, but, Riam, you have a guest."

Riam stood, frowning. "Who is it?"

Amity shrugged. "I apologize, but I don't know who it is. No one does."

Riam pulled the door open then brushed past Amity. Sid stood in the hall behind her. Sid growled under his breath. He didn't like anyone touching her, but he wouldn't tell anyone the details. Riam followed Sid into the main room.

Standing in the center of the room, in the middle of a house full of Slayers, a tall woman stood in a long, black, hooded robe. She lifted her pale face to Riam. Her eyes were midnight black. She was breathtakingly beautiful — the way a savage was in your darkest of nightmares, the way a bear was majestic before it ripped your fucking head off.

"Riam, I heard your call for aid," she said. Her voice was just over a whisper, but it rolled across the room like a scream. "My name is Bellum. If you prefer, you may call me Strain, the first born."

Chapter Nine

Riam had struggled to step through his fellow Slayers when he'd come into the room. In the middle stood the woman with her hands raised in the air, looking calmer than she should, given the guns pointed at her head. Her arms and legs were strapped with knives of different sizes, guns dangled from her hips and ribs, and a few wooden spikes were strapped across her chest for good measure. She had come prepared. But something about her told Riam that she didn't need a single one of those weapons to fight her way out.

A few inches shy of six feet tall, the woman called Bellum stared forward to Riam, as though she'd been waiting for only him. Her eyes tracked him as he pushed through his housemates, making his way to the front of the group.

Riam knew that look all too well. She had already eyed the Slayers, finding a way out should this go south in a heartbeat. He knew, from his own experience, that she'd have come up with a dozen different ways to kill most of the people in the room and a dozen more to get her ass to safety. It was exactly what he did when he walked into any given room. *Assess the risk and always have a plan B.*

Bellum looked to the women in the group, watching how closely the men stood next to them. If Bellum was anything like Riam, she would know to wound the women first. The men would react to help them before they moved in on the enemy. Love was mankind's greatest strength and biggest weakness. If Bellum were the warrior Riam thought she was, they were either in a heap of shit or worse – dead.

Bellum took one step forward. Her hands were still up

like she was waving a white flag. Riam lifted his gun slowly, aiming at her kneecap. He could feel the power rolling off her like a heat wave. Unlike the others who were aiming at her head, Riam knew none of them would tag her with a kill shot. She wouldn't have walked in here if she was that vulnerable. No one was that stupid. So he aimed to take her down, not out. Warrior or not, everyone reacted to pain and most needed their kneecaps to run away. *Here's hoping she's like everyone else.*

"How did you find this place?" Riam asked, staring into her midnight-black eyes.

They were the same eyes as Strain, only more. She was much more powerful than the current Strain but she left the same taste on the back of his tongue. There was something else in the air, something different. She tasted like power but also held the taste of defeat, the same flavor he'd swallowed down at the end of every war won. She was carrying a personal failure.

Riam caught Sid moving out of the corner of his eye. Sid stepped up beside Amity, touching her arm and guiding her back and away from the group. Amity had been inching her way forward, step by step, since Riam had walked into the room. She had studied Bellum, but not in fear. Amity looked curious. Then again, everyone was curious. *What the hell would a Strain be doing at the compound?* Amity glanced over to Riam and shrugged, as if she'd heard what Riam had thought. Riam looked to Des, who shook her head. Clearly she didn't know why Bellum was there either.

"I suggest you starting talking before someone's finger twitches and blows your brains all over the floor," Riam said, knowing she wouldn't believe what he was saying. Not even he believed a Slayer would accidentally shoot her. But he would, on purpose, in a heartbeat.

"As I said, I'm here to help. Finding you wasn't difficult. You don't exactly look over your shoulder on your way back from a hunt," Bellum said, then looked to Des. "She leaves a hint of herself every time she touches someone.

I merely had to follow it. If I can follow it, my father can follow it. And unlike me, he will kill you all."

Cael stepped in front of Des, his face twisting into anger. Protective just didn't cover it.

"I've been following you all for months." Bellum said. She grinned as she watched that knowledge sink into everyone in the room. She tilted her head, looking to Bane, who was growling. "Before you even think of it, drunk little hound, if I wanted you all dead, you'd simply be dead. I'd have taken you out the moment you proposed to that dog at the club. Why would I bother with this chitchat?"

Riam cleared his throat, shaking his head at Bane, but keeping his eyes on Bellum. He didn't bother asking how she'd known they were at the club. He had a feeling he'd already met her in the alley. "You say you've come to help. How?"

"I'm not going to stand here all night with my hands up. Call them off and we can talk...or I walk," she answered. "If I walk, this was all for nothing and we all will die. I have risked too much to die — not now and not for any of you."

"She's right," Sid spoke up. "If she wanted you all dead, you'd be dead. You'd have kicked it months ago when she first started following us."

Riam lowered his gun and gave her a nod. She lowered her arms. The rest of the room lowered their guns then started clearing out, leaving the senior Slayers. Riam looked at Sid. Sid had seen her coming, but he hadn't. He knew what this meant. Bellum was on the same path as Riam.

It had taken nearly fifteen minutes for the Slayers to put down their guns and allow Bellum to lower her hands. No one trusted someone who smelled like the very darkness they were hunting. Riam didn't fault them, and from the look on Bellum's face, she didn't either. She had walked straight into the proverbial bear den and was handling it pretty well, considering every bear was awake and inches from her throat.

Now that things had calmed, Riam stood at the twenty-foot wooden table with his most senior comrades circled around. Bellum stood at the far end, with her hands pressed flat on the surface, leaning forward, staring at Riam.

"We don't have much time, Riam. My father has one of your kind. You know what that means." Bellum spoke, her voice carrying, hitting him in the chest, reminding him of the suffering Sasha was enduring.

No one else spoke. They stared with their mouths agape. No one in the compound knew what Riam was, aside from Sid, who knew just about everything there was to know about everyone walking the earth.

Riam nodded. Sasha had felt familiar when he had found her at Strain's compound. Her eyes were mirrors of his, a deep pool filled with regrets, near misses and sadness. She had felt like home, from long ago.

"As you well know, my father can only produce new offspring with a Seer."

"Seer?" Bane asked, still slurring, gripping the table as though he were about to fall off the edge of the world.

Bellum jerked her head, staring at Bane then back to Riam. "They don't know what you are? Why the fuck would you keep that from them?"

"It was not for them to know," Riam answered.

"Um, is anyone going to tell me what the hell a Seer is?" Bane piped up again, hiccupping and moaning as he held his stomach.

"Long story short… Before there was heaven and earth, sin and Hades, there was nothing. Pure darkness. A vast space of not a goddamn thing." Bellum paced back and forth at the head of the table, pausing every so often in thought. She titled her head from side to side. "In that nothing, Riam's people were created, little glints of light. They were made long before the angels and journeyers, long before demons and sin. His people were used to fight off the darkness. It was their sole purpose. Heaven and earth – along with mankind – was created from the light left behind."

Bellum looked at Sid as if she were expecting the Watchyr

to say something. That man was more tight-lipped than Riam was. Sid raised his eyebrows and stared at the ceiling.

Bellum frowned then nodded, as though she understood his silence. "Then, after a few thousand years, Riam's people had done what every other creation did throughout history. They were given free will and they fucked themselves royally with it. They were punished for what they had done, going against their gods. They had created new life with humans, something prohibited by the Orygin. They were struck down, leaving one survivor who procreated with a Sibyl. Riam is of that direct line, a Seer, birthed of Laocoon, a Priest of Apollo. The Genesys can procreate with only their line, as they both come from the line of darkness. Did I leave anything out, Riam?"

Riam shook his head. She had said more in a few minutes than he ever had over the course of his entire existence. "I think you nailed it."

"There are only two direct descendants of the darkness, angels and demons. Each line created new life. The Orygin tried to restore the balance by deactivating the gene passed down throughout generations of mankind. The Genesys reactivated that gene."

"Are you saying that Riam is an angel?" Bane asked with a hint of laughter.

"No more than I am, little drunkard," Sid answered. "There are only two pure lines, Angels and Demons. The Genesys was created by the light and dark procreating. Riam's people were created when the light produced life with mankind. The rest of the irregulars were a result of light or dark breeding with mankind."

"It was ruled that light and dark could not produce a half-breed. There have only been two to survive to adulthood — Desdemona and my father. Prophetycs are now killed at birth," Bellum said, looking at Des sympathetically. "It is too risky to have someone with that kind of power out in the world."

Des looked to Sid, her eyes wide open. "Were you

supposed to kill me?"

Bellum answered for Sid. "I came for you. He stopped me. I've spent my life in exile, hunting irregulars who are from the darkness."

Sid winked at Des, but he couldn't answer the question. Some secrets weren't meant to be told. Sid was bound, clearly Bellum wasn't.

"This is the closest I've ever gotten to you, without your Watchyr sinking a blade into my chest. Once you hit maturity, Sidriel and I struck a deal. If you chose the path of evil, he'd kill you himself. If you chose the path of light, I would help keep you alive," Bellum said, giving Sid a nod. "You've done well, Watchyr."

"As have you, little war," Sid answered back.

"You've been a busy target to protect," Bellum said, looking at Des. "But if you can help me take down my father, it was time well spent."

Des looked to Sid, as though she wanted more information, but then dropped the topic. She was one of the few who didn't push Sid too far. She knew he would say only what he could. Riam knew Des well enough to know she was okay with her Watchyr taking her out if she went dark. She, like the rest of the Slayers, would sooner die than become what they all hunted.

Bellum left the topic alone and focused on the real threat, which was not Des. "My father has Sasha, the woman left behind when Nerissa was rescued."

"Do you know where she is?" Riam asked, his muscles tensing at the comment about Sasha being left behind. They didn't *leave* her behind, not willingly — or so that's what he told himself.

Bellum nodded. "Yes, and I know where my brother is, as do you. I want in. I want a piece of this. I've been in hiding long enough. Let me in and I'll kill my brother and my father."

"Tell me where Sasha is," Riam demanded. "Once she is safe, we can talk shop."

Bellum shook her head. "I want in or I walk. Now or never. I'm not putting my ass on the line for nothing. Tick-tock, my friends. We don't have much time. He needs her to agree to lie with him. Call it a failsafe from the big kahuna upstairs. Only the willing can be used to bring forth life with the doomed. She must be aware and give consent, or the child will be stillborn. But I promise you this. He will give her whatever she wants for this to happen. He will promise her the moon and stars and he will make true on his word, in his own way. She's been on a warpath for my brother. My father will hand him over, and we are royally fucked. He will create a new Strain, and he won't make the same mistakes he did with my brother and I. There will be no free will, no soul, no conscience—just darkness. With each Strain, he learns where he went wrong. The third child will be worse than the humans' version of the antichrist."

Bane leaned forward, his drunken glow strong in the air. "You smell exactly like how tears taste to my wolf, like when you're fighting someone and they're losing but won't stay down and they cry, trying to get back up. That's what you smell like. The person who is desperate to get back up."

Bellum turned her eyes to Bane, every emotion void from her face. "I am desperate for Riam's help. What are you?"

Bane growled from deep within his soul, his wolf sending a warning to Bellum. "I am the wolf who will hunt you down and slowly rip your fucking head off if you harm him."

Before an argument could erupt, Sid touched Riam's shoulder. "I'll watch over her."

"You may be leading your father or brother to us right this second." Riam stared at Bellum for a hard minute. "I don't trust you."

"I wouldn't trust my kind either. I am a Strain. I am an abomination. I'd have killed myself years ago if I wouldn't end up back with my father. I am cursed. The only thing I can do is take him out and rid this world of his wicked darkness," Bellum answered. "If they could track me, I'd have been dead long ago. Neither of them can find me. When my father exiled me, he tried to wipe my memory. He severed all ties then dumped me on my ass. My memories were not gone as he'd hoped, and I had to learn how to shield against him."

Cael's sigh brought everyone's attention to the side of the table. "I don't like this."

"When this is over, you may take my life," Bellum responded, her eyes downcast at the floor.

"We don't murder people," Cael said, sounding insulted.

Bellum lifted her eyes, tears rolling down her cheeks. "I beg you to take my life, once they are gone. I will *not* become my father or my brother. With them gone, I will *not* return to the darkness. If I could do it myself, I would, but suicides go to Hades. I believe I've lived enough lifetimes in my own Hades. I do not need to go to another one."

"You wishing for death doesn't make me trust you. Hell, most of us here have wished for it a time or two," Riam said, staring her in the eyes, trying to figure her out.

She nodded. "I was the one who helped you, Riam. I sent the letter. I gave you the stone to ward against the darkness. I stopped you in the alley and gave you my memories of my brother. I've spent every fucking night outside, in your back fields, shielding this compound from my father, my brother and anyone else looking for you. If I wanted you dead, I'd have simply made my brother or father aware of your location, then let them handle the rest. I've sacrificed everything to be here."

Cael ordered a two-man guard on Bellum — Bane and Sid — at all times. She wouldn't blink without someone seeing it. No one was happy about having her in the compound. Riam wasn't happy or unhappy about it. He didn't trust her but he needed her. He didn't dislike her for who she was, but he didn't plan on inviting her for tea, either.

With Bellum on board, Riam cut to the chase. "Where is she?"

"She is inside my father. He is the shadow and darkness that holds her. We will need my brother to get to my father, in order to get my father out in the open," Bellum replied then smiled. "I thought you'd all like to know that my brother has been stripped of all his abilities. He's human, through and through — a punishment from our father."

Cael grinned. "Well, that made my day."

"When I saw him, I thought something was off. He's being referred to by his human name, and that must be why," Riam explained, remembering the moment he'd watched Strain step out of the club. He'd looked weak, like a human who had lived inside an eight ball of blow for a little too long.

Bellum nodded and turned back to Riam. "We need my brother alive, for now. He and I can draw my father out."

"Alive...for now," Cael agreed. "Dawn is coming. Everyone rest up. We head out when darkness falls."

"Darkness always falls," Bellum mumbled. "It's everywhere."

Riam escorted Bellum to a bedroom. He and Sid stood inside the plain room that held one double bed, a nightstand with a lamp and a four-drawer dresser. Bellum removed her robe and slowly stripped off her weapons. Each one clunked onto the bare wood floor. She wouldn't be allowed to keep them, although she could kill them all with or without them.

Turning her back to the men, she unzipped her leather jacket and tossed it behind her back to Riam. Her leather pants were next, leaving her standing in a white spaghetti strap shirt and white boyshorts. She pulled off her shirt and tossed it on the floor beside her naked feet. When she turned, her cheeks were flushed red and her eyes glittered. She extended her arms and closed her eyes.

Her body was covered in aged scars. Lash marks marred her back and legs. Over top of the scars were tattoos.

"I was a disappointment to my father. I'd never do as commanded. To his anger, I was born with a soul and a conscience. I couldn't indiscriminately kill innocents. At first, he tried to beat my morals out of me. When that failed, he tried to rip them out of me by way of an oiled whip. But eventually, I rose up against him. I almost killed him but I hesitated. I couldn't kill him then, and you have all paid for that failure." Bellum opened her eyes and small tears rolled down her cheeks.

Riam picked her shirt off of the floor, feeling like an asshole. She wasn't the one who'd failed them all. It was the Seers that had caused this entire problem. "Please, put your clothes back on."

"I wear these scars proudly, Riam. Each one reminds me of when I wouldn't kill an innocent. Each scar is a soul I sacrificed for. There is no shame in that," Bellum answered, but pulled her shirt on anyway.

"The tattoos?" Riam asked, staring at the markings in two separate languages that looked familiar. One was Egyptian and one he couldn't place.

"Tamil, one of the oldest languages known to man, and Egyptian. They are wards to keep my father and brother from finding me. One is to ward against the darkness and one is to ward against the light. Both sides want me dead."

Riam and Sid left Bellum in her bedroom. Bane took up post outside of her door.

"She's a ghost. We know nothing about her, aside from what she's told us. This better not be a waste of our time," Riam said, standing beside Bane.

"Welcome to the bottom of the totem pole," Bane cracked, "where everything sounds like a bad idea because you have no real say in the matter."

Sid took up shop across the hall, leaning into the wall and sliding down to his rear. "Cheer up, ole chap."

"You said you'd keep an eye on her. You're the one that volunteered. Why?" Riam asked.

Sid shrugged and motioned like he was locking his lips. Riam groaned and walked away, ending up on the floor in his bedroom.

Chapter Ten

"Don't be a little bitch, Riam. I've seen your balls. They're bigger than this," Bellum said, pouring out a bag of salt on the ground. "Man the fuck up and get in the circle with me."

It was Cael's brilliant idea to pair the two for the night. As usual, everyone was out on duty, combing the streets for the Order and cleaning up the messes Deagon — aka Strain — was creating.

The moment Bellum and Cael were out of sight, she'd sprung her master plan on Riam. Together, they would enter the darkness, Riam protected by the stone and Bellum covered by her tats. At first, Riam was down with the idea, but the closer they got to the warehouse on the outskirts of Van City, the less this seemed like a good idea. The little hairs on the back of his neck were dancing, sending off warning flares. If they had a voice, they'd be telling his feet to beat pavement.

"I've been inside the darkness. I can't move or speak. I couldn't find her." Riam reminded Bellum of his last stint inside the Genesys.

Bellum eyed up her circle of salt, dropping the leftover half bag on the outside of the ring of protection. The circle did nothing to stop her father from pulling their arms off like petals on a daisy, but it kept the rest of the creepy-crawlies from biting off a chunk. "You didn't have the stone then, either. I've been inside of my father's darkness many times. It takes time for him to feel me. The same will be for you. He cannot control what he cannot see. Now man the fuck up and let's get this shit show on the road. We have no idea of Sasha's condition. If she's suffered her first death, getting her out before the sun is up is probably a grand plan. That's all we need...to pull her out then toast her ass."

Riam stepped inside the circle then knelt on the floor, breathing deeply. He looked up to Bellum. "Why does Sid call you 'little war'?"

"Bellum loosely translates into the word 'war' in Latin. He's called me 'little war' since the first day he met me."

"I'm surprised he didn't kill you for going after Des. No one touches Des."

Bellum knelt with a grin. "There were a few times I thought it was the end. But each time, he pulled the blade out of my chest and walked away, warning me. It takes a lot to kill me, but Sid's stubborn enough to wait it out. The last time I went for Des, everything changed. I found her in some rat shack foster home. She was standing in front of two small children, protecting them. She held a fork in her hand, going up against a two-hundred-pound man. She was willing to kill the guy with a fucking fork for two kids she'd only met earlier at dinner. I listened to her pray for help, pray to the Orygin, pray for strength to endure. When he took the fork from her, she bargained. She would be his little toy for the night and every night to come, if he left the two children alone. He agreed and Des played victim."

Riam closed his eyes, sending out a thank you to the Orygin for people like Desdemona. "Des would trade every feather on her back for the innocent."

"I know, so I went back. I killed the man, slowly. I waited for him to head to the liquor store then I lured him into an alley. Just before I took his life, I whispered her name into his ear. I wanted him to know why I was killing him, why he'd earned his death. As you know, I made a deal with Sid after that. If she stayed on the path of light, I'd help him keep her alive."

"How the hell did you end up on this side of the line? No offense meant."

Bellum shrugged. "I don't know. I mean, it would be

easier to not have a conscience, to have been able to do as my father commanded. Life could have been glorious without a soul."

Riam shook his head. "Losing a soul is the most painful experience. Every wound that pulls you and your soul apart is like a tiny death. Just ask Des."

"And you, Riam. When I gave you my memories, I received a few in return. It was not on purpose, but it happens during the exchange. I have seen moments where you grieved the wounds on your soul. I have seen you blame yourself for the creation of my father."

"You have no right to those memories, nor do I wish for you to discuss them."

Bellum squeezed her eyes tighter. He knew she was preparing for the journey just as he had previously. "As I have heard you all say, time and time again, you cannot run from fate. Fate happens with or without your aid. My father would have been birthed, regardless of your own creation or the choices you made. It would have happened, Riam. That's all I mean. You can beat yourself up for it if you would like, but you are no more to blame that I."

Riam's first instinct was to shut her down. But he swallowed it and nodded. "Thank you, Bellum. I appreciate your words."

She laughed. "No, you don't, you fuckin' liar."

"Okay, not really, but thank you just the same."

"Are you ready for this, Riam? Are you ready to step into the darkness? If you cannot do it, step out of the circle and I will do this for you. Either way, we must go now. I can feel my father's impatience with her. She has not given consent, yet, but it's close."

Riam closed his eyes and breathed deeply. "I'm ready."

Bellum clasped Riam's hand, looping a rope around his wrist then hers. She reminded him to keep the rope on at all times. They couldn't separate or he would be left behind. Her mission was to get Sasha and only Sasha. She wouldn't stick around for him. The Genesys couldn't use Riam for anything more than a punching bag. Bellum wasn't about to risk it all to keep him from a few kicks. Riam was on board with the plan. He'd sooner have Sasha out and safe than have it all blown to shit.

In agreement, Bellum began chanting in a language Riam did not fully understand. It was a mixture of multiple tongues, most of which were long forgotten. He picked up the odd word here and there, words meaning protection and darkness. She was asking someone to protect them as they entered the darkness. *Nothing can protect us in the darkness*, Riam thought.

It was like a slow sunset into complete darkness, only he knew it was happening in an instant. It was similar to pouring ice cold water into boiling hot water while sitting in the pot with it. Even with his eyes closed, he noticed the change in darkness. Somehow black could become blacker. His mind raced to catch up, unable to understand the instant change in temperature. His body grew heavier, yet lighter. He felt like he was glued to the floor, his bones were lined with lead. Yet his arms felt weightless. Everything was a contradiction inside the void of the Genesys.

Bellum pulled on the rope, saying nothing, drawing his mind forward to focus on her. He could have gotten lost in the thoughts of where he was. The rope snapped his mind into the game at hand. They were hidden from the Genesys, but eventually, he would feel the difference in his darkness. He would feel someone else was present, would clue in. Similar to being watched, you couldn't see who watched you, but you could feel them.

On the way to the warehouse, Bellum had been explicitly clear with getting in and out. She called it a bank job. It was like they had one minute until the alarms would go off and the po-po were on their way. One minute inside would feel different to both Bellum and Riam, but each second that ticked by would feel like centuries to their sanity. She'd said that no one left the void without needing therapy or a bullet. She'd give Sasha the option. Sometimes therapy did nothing to keep you from clawing out your eyes as soon as the sun went down and the darkness came back for you.

Riam followed the tug of the rope, trying to listen for signs of life. He heard nothing, not even the beat of his own heart. The darkness felt like wet smog, tasting like pollution and an abandoned meat market, fully stocked. Each breath tasted worse than the last. The disgusting darkness ate up sound like a starved animal.

Riam's ears twitched and he pulled on the rope, stopping Bellum. She'd heard it as well, pulling back against Riam. His paced quickened, as Bellum pulled Riam toward the noise. He could tell she knew her way around. She moved as though she had perfect sight inside the void.

"I will *never* agree!" Sasha's voice cut through the smog of the darkness and hit Riam.

Bellum pushed her hand into Riam's chest and leaned into his ear. In a whisper he had to strain to hear, she said, "Riam, we have one shot at this. It's a grab and go."

He nodded quickly then they moved in. Riam could feel the change in the air like someone else was there. He could feel the heat from her body, smell the tears she was crying and hear her murmurs as she wept. It made his stomach roll.

As planned, Bellum and Riam grabbed Sasha together. Riam grabbed her feet, which meant Bellum was up by her head. Sasha's body twitched under his grip. Before she could get out a scream, he knew Bellum would be covering Sasha's mouth. But through the mumbles, he could hear Sasha screaming for him, calling out Riam's name. It was clear that she'd known he would come for her. Bellum whispered a chant to return them all to the warehouse.

In blinding speed, they were thrown from the darkness. He opened his eyes. He was laying on his side with Sasha in front of him, screaming. Bellum was on her hands and knees, puking.

"Shut her the fuck up." Bellum gagged, in between her stomach evacuating.

Riam didn't bother trying to explain that they were the good guys or that she was safe. He didn't remind her of who he was and that he'd come for her. He didn't fill her head with bullshit about her rescue. She was too far gone to have heard a word. Bellum had given him a needle with a little sleepy-time med. He hadn't asked what it was. If she wanted Sasha dead, she'd have gone in and killed her alone. Hell, she'd have just left Sasha there and dealt with her when she was too far gone to have put up a fight.

Sasha was trying to crawl away on her hands and knees when Riam grabbed her ankle and jabbed the needle into her thigh. It didn't take long for the drugs to kick in. She had struggled while slowly lowering face-first to the floor. He felt like an asswipe, knowing she had fought for her survival, only to be overcome by a needle.

"Riam, we have to go — and now," Bellum said, moving to the front of the warehouse. "Riam, *now!*"

Riam glanced up at Bellum, blinking. He lifted Sasha into his arms then stood. "Let's rock."

Bellum shook her head. "She can't come with us, not back to the compound. My father has marked her. Look at her stomach. He can track her, no matter where we take her."

Riam moved Sasha in his arms, exposing her nude stomach. It looked like blood poisoning. Long red lines covered her abdomen, running down her thighs and up to her chest. Whatever The Genesys had done to her had caused massive septicemia. Looking up at her face, Riam could see how sick she was. Her skin was pasty white, almost gray. Her lips had a cold blue tinge, even though she was flaming hot to the touch. She looked like she was near death.

"Think of my father as bacteria. His touch can infect. He does this to force their hand to agree. He pollutes them with the Strain, his evil. He is inside of her, Riam. If we take her to your compound, through her, he will find you all. He will kill all of you or he will use the Slayers to force her to procreate. Either way, we're all fucked," Bellum said, her face snarling into a hateful glare. "Riam, you must take her life, both of them. Give her the mercy of death. She wouldn't want to be the reason you all died, and she wouldn't want to give birth to another Strain. Do this so she doesn't have to kill herself when she comes back an infected Vampyre."

Riam blinked, staring at Bellum. His brain struggled to reason with what she was saying. *Kill her?* They'd just rescued her.

"I can't just kill her," Riam said, shaking his head.

"She will come back, Riam, infected with my father. Do you want her to spread that infection? Everyone she feeds from will be turned into a form of Proletaryan, only worse. Do you remember the Upyr Vampyres? The most savage of Vampyre, they fed on children and could not be controlled. My father's infection was the cause of that. My father creates monsters, nothing more."

The folklore behind the Upyr Vampyre said they were the only full Vampyre that could face the sun without burning. They had fed on women and children, taking out entire communities and schools. They were why Vampyres were feared. They were what nightmares were made of. The Seers had been dispatched to extinguish the Upyr. The Seers had lost almost a dozen people during that hunt. No one had seen where they had come from or what caused them. They chalked it up to a mutation in the irregular gene.

"I can't do this," Riam whispered, backing away from Bellum with Sasha in his arms. "There has to be another way."

Bellum stepped forward, pulling a blade from her thigh holster. "If you cannot, I will do it for you, Riam. You do not have to carry the burden of her death. I will carry it for you. It is but a small thing for me to do."

Riam took another step backward. "Don't do this, Bellum. I swear to you I will kill you if you touch her. Please, don't make me kill you."

Bellum muffled a deep scream. "Fuck, Riam. Fuck."

"There has to be a cure," Riam said then set Sasha on the

floor. He pulled out his phone to call Sid. But in true Sid fashion, he opened the door to the warehouse and stepped inside. That was Sid, always two steps ahead — there before you could call out his name.

With an ear-to-ear smile, he laughed. "Well, aren't you two fucked six ways from Sunday?"

Sid lifted his fingers to his mouth and piped out a high-pitched whistle. The door opened again and Bane stepped through, followed by Cael, Des, Amity, Zylan and Neri.

Neri was dressed in scrubs and carrying her medical bag. She didn't stop to ask questions or give Riam the third degree about doing this without having her standing by. Thinking back, Riam knew it would have been a better decision to have them all there. But again, he was thinking the risk was too great.

Neri jumped into action, her Fyrvor at her side, passing her equipment that she requested. Watching them always made Riam smile. They were one and the same, two peas in a pod. Zylan knew what Neri would ask for before it came out of her mouth.

Neri asked Bellum questions about Sasha and what the cause could be. From the look on her face, Riam knew Neri didn't like any of the answers. She drew blood and hissed, holding up the black-filled vial. Bane had taken a step back, noticeably smelling something in the air that no one else could smell. The deep red, almost black, that flowed out of her veins told Riam that Bellum was probably right. It was a deadly infection.

"Whatever it is, it is spreading and damn fast. I don't know how to stop it, Riam. I've never seen anything like this," Neri said, standing up in front of him. "I'm sorry, Riam. I can make her comfortable, but that's all I can do. She will die from this and I don't think her first death will cure whatever is running through her veins."

Des knelt beside Sasha and touched her hand. Des twitched, her eyes sprung wide open and her jaw dropped. She shook her head back and forth, tears rolled from her eyes. "Sadness and pain, such unbelievable anguish. Oh my God, too much pain. Riam, she is aware of what is happening to her."

Before Cael could grab Des and pull her into the protection of his arms, Amity touched Des. Amity could heal others, pushing her soul from her body and allowing it to mend the broken, but it came at a price. It could end her life. She had already given her first death to save Neri. She'd never recover from a second.

Sid jumped from the group and pulled Amity away, shaking his head. "Amity, no."

"I must try, Sidriel. It is who I was born to be, a healer. I may be able to help her." Amity spoke softly.

Sid was overly protective of Amity, always on guard when she was around. Riam didn't ask him questions. If Sid wanted the others to know why, he'd tell them.

"No, there is nothing you can do, not this time. There is nothing any of us here can do." Sid said, looking back to Riam. "No one *here* can help her."

Riam nodded. Sid has just given him another clue. He was torn. He had to leave Sasha, to go for help, but he didn't want to. For the first time in his life, he was uncertain and caught between a rock and a hard place.

"We will watch over her, Riam, as if she were your Fyrvor," Cael said, stepping up. "I will guard her with my life."

Bellum growled. "Fuck. We need to get her into the middle of the salt circle. Des, I will need you to use your abilities to cloud her mind, put her on a beach, remove any memory of Riam and me. Neri, pump her full of as much painkiller as possible without killing her. Keep her riding that edge, life and death. We need to do whatever we can to keep my father from sensing her and finding her."

"Go, Riam. You have one hour," Sid said, giving him a wink.

In one hour, there would be nothing Riam could do to save Sasha. There would be nothing left to save. Then he'd have to do the unthinkable. He'd have to kill her. That was if the Genesys didn't beat him to the punch. She had fought tooth and nail to survive in a world that had taken everything from her, but Riam would kill her if he had to.

Chapter Eleven

Riam hadn't bothered to make his way back to the compound. He didn't need a telephone to contact a healer, either. He'd found a quiet space, far from the reaches of the city. The lush green grass filled his lungs and reminded him of times he appreciated, memories that wars had not yet destroyed. The sky above was clear, exposing the stars and the beauty they resembled. He focused on his surroundings, trying to remove the tension in his shoulders. He let go of his worry for Sasha and grounded himself in the moment, letting the cool breeze pull away the fear held deep in his bones.

Riam closed his eyes, kneeling in the dewy grass after pouring out a thin circle of salt. He'd waited for his hands to stop shaking then sent out a call for aid. He pushed his mind out, following the pull of his people. He hadn't asked for aid from anyone, ever. He was praying they would hear his call and, at the very least, coming poking around out of curiosity.

"Riam."

One word and he wanted to puke.

He opened his eyes, standing an inch from his five-foot circle of salt, stood the Aegys of his people, their guardian. They didn't have a leader. They never had. They no longer considered themselves an army, and he wondered why she was the one who had answered his call. She wasn't completely there, not in a physical form. It was an impression of her, in his mind. But that was enough to make him want to pull back and wash his hands of it.

"Myranda," Riam said, that one word feeling like a

lifetime of heated and hated discussions.

Myranda was the first-born daughter of his people. Her birthing parents were long past. She was the eldest of his race and hadn't come knocking often. In fact, he'd never received a house call from her before. She had retired into seclusion following the disbandment of the armies. He wondered why she, of all people, would be the one to answer his call for help. He'd never banked on her being willing.

"I felt your pain. It has been many years since I have felt you in my mind. Our people are returning home since the wars have begun with the Genesys." She answered as if she had heard his thoughts.

Her voice reminded him of lying in the sun beside a gentle stream. She was calmness. Everything about her told him to break his circle of protection and let her in. But he knew better. She was the calm before the storm. To break his circle would give away his location, and he wasn't willing to do that—not yet. Myranda was only there in thought, but that scared him enough to be cautious. She could not see where he was or he was sure she would have been standing face to face with him.

"I require a healer," Riam said, feeling his skin crawl with her being that close. "Sasha, a Seer, is mortally wounded. She will not heal this injury. An infection, given to her by the Genesys, has taken root."

Myranda nodded her head, her long, wavy-brown locks bouncing off her shoulders. Myranda, who Riam had once thought was the epitome of beauty, repulsed him now. She reminded him of everything he hated about himself. All the gory details of his life could be found inside her.

"We are aware of Sasha and all she has done. She has broken the one vow we all have taken. She manipulated the future to serve her personal needs. She created a path that brought her to her partner and children. This path was taken back. We will allow destiny to run its course," Myranda said, her voice void of emotion as though she were reading a shopping list.

Riam looked up and glared. He knew Sasha's partner and children had been killed, but, until that moment, he hadn't fully understood why. Now, he had the answers to why her wicked hate ran so deep. Fate had taken back what it was owed, but it didn't lessen the pain it would have caused her.

Riam sighed, his heart heavy for Sasha. "We are the only chance she has. I can bring her back, Myranda. Give her a chance. All she knows is hate and sadness. Give me a chance to help her heal her soul."

Myranda shook her head. "We cannot risk it. She has done far too much damage already."

"That is not your decision to make, Myranda. It's not up to you to assign death to anyone. It is part of our vow. You, yourself, are going against the vow, by standing by and doing nothing," Riam spat his words, angry. "It is our duty to help, not to harm. By doing nothing, when you know you can help… It goes against everything we were meant to be."

"Do not lecture me, little one. I am not going against my vow. I am simply exercising my free will and choosing not to help her."

"Then that is your choice, not the choice of my people." Riam punched his fists into the ground, feeling his muscles bulge in anger. "I demand to speak to the council."

Myranda inched forward, smiling. Her smile showed the hint of her fangs. "They are already listening."

Riam jerked his head up, unable to see them. It didn't matter to him. He spoke out anyway. "Please, help me. Just help me, not her. Give me the tools I need to help her. I'm begging you. I have always been a loyal subject and have carried out every order without fail. Help me. Someone… please."

"What about the balance, Riam?" Myranda asked.

Riam swallowed hard and thought of Layla. He wondered what she would say, kneeling in his place. He knew his sister had a heart of gold and a soul so pure it sparkled clear. She was different from the rest of the Seers. She honored all life and hated being forced to defend herself against those they went up against. The only time she brought mankind to their knees was under the threat of her own death. But in the last war, she hadn't defended herself. Riam had watched her allow the wooden spike to pierce her chest. Layla had stood with her arms open, nodding with a smile, and she had welcomed the death. She was done — done killing, done fighting against her fellow man. When the wooden death came down upon her, she forgave the man who took her life. She had been his sister — honorable, forgiving and kind.

"I would give myself. I would give my first and second life, to save hers. I would die to save her. Take it. Take whatever you want from me. It's yours," Riam said. The truth of his words finally warmed parts of him that he hadn't known were frozen. A place in his heart that had been empty and cold pulsed for the first time since he'd said goodbye to his sister.

Riam felt a warm hand on his shoulder and he knew it was Bane.

"I will give my life for her. I will give you my wolf," Bane said, kneeling down beside Riam. Bane couldn't see what Riam saw, but his wolf would hear it and sense it.

Riam turned to his comrade, smiling, with tears in his eyes. "I couldn't ask that of you."

"And you didn't. We are a team, Riam. You are not alone. You will never be alone again." Bane spoke, holding his head high. "Did you hear me? I give my wolf for the Seer, Sasha."

Riam looked back to Myranda and spoke to his people. "Please, someone help me."

"*Us*," Bane corrected Riam. "*We* call on you to aid *us*."

A young woman stepped into view. Riam knew her. She was a healer of his people. Opal was her name. She was younger than Riam but had the wisdom of more years than he. He had met her on the battlefield. She was as courageous as they came. She darted in and out of war zones and crawled through broken glass and rock to give help to anyone who needed it, including those who Myranda called the enemy. Opal was neutral. Her oath to heal was a blanket for all life. Neri reminded Riam of Opal. Neri had crawled through war to save souls. Riam could see why Zylan was crazy for her.

"I will help him, Myranda," Opal said.

Myranda glared. "We do not meddle, never again."

Opal smiled, nodding her head. "I agree. We do not meddle with destiny. If it is the will of the Orygin for Sasha to die, she will simply die and nothing I do to save her will change that. You are blind, Myranda, blind to why we are here. I will help Riam, with your approval or not. As you exercise your right to free will, so will I."

Myranda reached toward Riam, with an ugly look twisted on her face, her fangs exposed and shining in the light of the moon. Riam could feel her hate for him. He knew she despised him for leaving them, for starting the dismantlement of the Seers. She'd lost her power the moment he'd thrown his sword to the ground then walked away. When he left, the others followed, and she'd carried a flame of hate for him ever since. He knew she wasn't going to help him, because she wanted him to hurt as badly as she did. This had nothing to do with right and wrong. It was simply wicked vengeance.

As Myranda reached forward with her crimson-painted nails, Bane's wolf lunged from his body, tearing at Myranda's hand. A ghost of a wolf bit down on her hand, landing in front of Riam and Bane, growling. His hairs stood on end, his teeth smashing together, nipping at the air between them. There would be no further warning from Bane's animal.

"Holy shit, holy shit, holy shit," Bane rambled. "Riam, can you see that? My wolf, he's out, but I'm still here. What the fuck is going on? Oh God, it feels awful. Am I dying?"

Bane reached out, making contact with his wolf and pulling his hand back, staring at it.

"It's okay, young wolf," Opal said, stepping forward, ahead of Myranda. The wolf growled at her. Once she placed her hand on his shoulder, the wolf sat and whimpered, rolling his head into her body. "I am a friend, dear wolf. I bring you no harm. I am on my way, Riam. I will follow the wolf back."

Riam pulled his mind from his people, seeing the look fade on Myranda's face. So much hate had been housed inside her, but he didn't blame her. He knew what hate did to people. He was walking proof, as were most of his fellow Slayers.

Riam kicked the edge of the circle then sat in silence for a moment, thankful for Opal.

"Holy fucking shit, Riam. What the fuck? What's happening?" Bane yelled, clawing at his chest. "Where's my wolf? I can feel him, but he's not here. What's going on?"

Bane started screaming, his nails digging into his arms. Riam had seen this happen before—a Therian separated from their animal. They went crazy. It was like declawing a cat, removing what they are. Most cats went batshit after having their fingertips cut off. And like a cat, Therians show their underground parking garage filled with a rubber-room style of craziness.

Bane was on the verge of losing his mind. His wolf wasn't just separated from him. It was out in the world with a Seer touching it. Bane would feel what his wolf was feeling, taste the air and smell the same smells. But Bane would feel completely apart from it. It was like a split personality on crack.

"It will be okay, Bane. You're not alone," Riam yelled over Bane's high-pitched screaming.

Bane quieted his screams but couldn't stop the shakes. He was going through something similar to severe life and death withdrawals. "It...was worth...this. It was worth...

I'm okay."

Bane's teeth chattered. His skin grew icy cold. Riam did the only thing he could think of. He climbed behind Bane and grabbed on to him. Riam waited with Bane for his wolf. Bane shivered, even though his body was blistering hot to the touch. Riam whispered to Bane, trying to keep his mind from plunging off the deep end.

"I can feel Opal coming, Bane. Just hold on," Riam whispered. "You did good, young pup. Hang in there."

Bane whispered, stretching his arms forward. Riam could see Opal running through the field, her almost-white hair flowing behind her in the wind. Bane's wolf was at her side. His wolf zeroed in then jumped toward his home inside Bane. His howl could be felt in Riam's marrow. Bane pulled away from Riam and rolled onto his back, his arms spread wide open. For a split second, while touching Bane, Riam could feel everything Bane was feeling. Normally, Riam guarded against feeling the emotions of his comrades, but in that instant, he could feel it all.

Bane would have freely sent his wolf to die, and his wolf would have gone willingly. Both were prepared to sacrifice themselves for the Slayers. The Slayers would never find a more loyal man and beast than Bane and his wolf. Willing or not, the sorrow Bane had felt, the moment his wolf was gone, was maddening. His mind couldn't come to grips with being completely alone. As soon as his wolf's paws touched home, Bane's body relaxed. Four minutes had passed, but to Bane, a lifetime of emptiness had gone by. And he'd do it again. Riam could feel it. Bane rolled to his side, hugging his chest, crying.

Opal knelt and touched Bane's cheek. "Your wolf would die a thousand deaths for you. It is a bond I have never felt before, between man and animal. When you meditate, allow your beast to sit beside you, and the bond will only grow. It will also give your mind time to grow used to you sending your wolf out."

Bane nodded his head, slowly sitting up. He touched his

arms and legs then patted his chest, smiling. His beast was home. With a help up from Riam, he grinned. "If you tell anyone I cried, I'll kick your nuts into your throat while you're sleeping."

"I'll always see you coming," Riam countered.

Bane gave Riam a playful glare. "I'll ply Sid with booze and have him do it for me. I know damn well you can't see Sid coming."

Riam grabbed Bane and hugged him. "Your secret is safe with me. I will never forget the sacrifice you made."

"I didn't sacrifice. They didn't take me up on it," Bane said, sounding happy that no one had accepted his offer.

Opal touched Bane's arm. "But you did. Whether we took it or not, you gave yourself willingly. It is an honorable sacrifice that no one will forget."

Riam and Bane brought Opal to the warehouse. Inside, the Slayers were at their posts, with Bellum in the middle, standing over Sasha with what looked like a small sword. Riam hadn't noticed it on her before and he made a note to pay closer attention to that woman.

Sid stepped up to Bane, patting him on the back. "Never doubt who you are, wolf."

"No 'young pup'?" Bane joked.

Sid gave him a hard look. "You, my friend, are no longer a pup. Well done."

Opal moved to the salt circle and cringed. Sasha was on her back, a shirt covering her breasts and one over her hips. Opal knelt down and placed her hands on Sasha's stomach, closing her eyes. She breathed in and out of her mouth, the smell turning even Riam's nose now.

He could smell her rotting from the inside out. It smelled of old meat, expired weeks ago. Sour death filled the air and made Riam's stomach roll. Bane had tried to step forward but backed up, holding his mouth and nose, shaking his head.

"Sidriel, may I ask for your assistance?" Opal asked, as though she knew him.

Sid stepped up to the circle. "What's up, Opal?"

"How do you know everyone?" Des asked, smiling.

Sid winked. "I get around."

Opal sighed, her face filled with concern. "I will remove her rot, but I will require a vessel for it."

Sid pushed up his sleeves and knelt beside Opal. "Let's get it done and over with."

Opal smiled. Her kind eyes were just for Sid. They had a history. Riam could see it in the way she looked at him. Sid winked at her, his smile meant to be kind and loving.

"In your words, Sidriel, this is gonna suck," Opal said, with a small laugh.

Sid looked to Riam. "When this is over, everyone needs to get the hell out of here. I'll be fine, but the Genesys will feel the power that comes with me. He will come looking."

"No, Sid, no fucking way." Des spoke up, stepping forward. She looked at Riam, her face twisted. "Find a different way, Riam. You're not taking my Watchyr from me to save Sasha. I'm sorry, but no."

"Calm down, crazy town. I'm not going anywhere. I'm the only one here who can take the rot and get rid of it. I'll take it and go home. A little dose of Elysium will cure this up like my last round with a prostitute."

Des' eyes glittered with tears. "Swear to me, Sid. Swear on my life that you're coming back."

Sid held out his pinky finger. "I swear. There's nothing in this world or the next that could keep me from your side."

Des stepped back into Cael's arms. Cael gave Sid a nod then took Des from the warehouse. Riam didn't understand how Cael didn't become jealous of Sid's and Des' relationship. The last time Cael and Des had had a disagreement, Cael found Sid in their closet, waiting to pounce on Cael if he overstepped. Sid walked in on them making love and even gave Cael pointers. Cael never once told Sid to back off. Each time Des had to touch someone to gain intel and was mind-fucked because of it, she went to Sid and not Cael. Cael waited patiently and would lift her from Sid's arms when she was ready.

Once, Zylan had asked Cael the question in Riam's presence. Cael defended Sid, saying Sid would die for Cael's one true love. He'd known going in that Des and Sid were a package deal. By loving Des, he ended up loving Sid. By being with Des, he could see parts of Sid that no one else could see. Des was a part of Sid and, in turn, he could find Sid inside her. If ever something had happened to Cael, Sid would make sure Des survived. Sid was the only one who loved Des as much, if not more, than Cael. And Cael was fine with that, even though Sid could be worse than burning blisters inside his rectum.

The warehouse cleared out, leaving Opal, Bellum, Riam and Sasha. Bane would wait outside, refusing to leave half of his team behind. Riam and Bellum would get Sasha out, Sid would go home and Opal would fhade.

Opal began. She held on to Sasha's and Sid's hands, pushing them together. Riam could not hear the words Opal spoke, but he could feel them touch his soul, healing the parts of him that had been wounded for centuries. Opal's gift of healing was soothing. She could heal the worst of Riam. He could feel it. The warehouse heated, the temperature rising to something that closely resembled Hades or a house fire. Sweat dripped into Riam's eyes as his blood felt like it was beginning to boil.

Sasha's eyes opened and her stomach jerked off the stone floor. Her mouth was stretched into a scream, but no noise could be heard. Sid's body mirrored Sasha's. He fell to his back, his stomach pitched to the roof. His jaw clenched shut as he muffled a scream. Both Sasha and Sid vibrated, their bodies hammering into the floor.

Riam watched as the red welts on Sasha's stomach disappeared, her injuries healing before his eyes. In turn, he knew that Sid was enduring the wounds and infection. The pain Sid was in was clear, with a twisted face and tears rolling from each eye. But he didn't scream out. He didn't call for help. That was Sid, always willing to suffer the greatest pain for humanity and even worse for his friends. He could put on whatever front he wanted, but Riam knew who Sid was, deep down. Sid carried his own cross on his back, lugging it around as though he deserved the punishment.

Opal let go of Sid's hand, backward crab crawling, trying to pull Sasha with her. Sasha was out cold, and Sid was writhing in pain.

"Go," Sid said through gritted teeth.

Riam snapped into action, yanking Sasha from the floor and lifting her over his shoulder. He grabbed Opal under her arm and pulled her to her feet. She was far too weak to fhade. Bellum was at the door, yelling for Bane.

Bane was in the warehouse and moved to Riam's side. Riam motioned toward Opal and without needing to say a word, Bane picked her up and moved away from Sid.

"Thank you," Riam said to Sid before leaving him in his pain.

"Run. He's coming!" Sid screamed. He closed his eyes and his body finally calmed. "Tell Des I'll be home soon. Tell her I won't break my promise."

They were out the door and into Bane's SUV within seconds. Bane peeled out of the lot, tires smoking. Bane drove a lot like Riam, pedal to the metal and no looking back. Riam trusted Bane's driving more than anyone else's. It was as if his wolf was miles up the road, sending back directions. Bane's road instincts were just that good.

Riam finally let out a deep breath, looking down into his arms. Sasha—who had once stood tall—was curled into the tiniest ball on his lap. Her features were finally smoothed out, no longer crunched into a painful glare of hate. He knew that when she woke, her anger would be back. But for this moment, she was the Sasha she had been long before the pain had taken her and twisted her into something the Genesys would want to breed with.

Chapter Twelve

There was a first time for everything in Deagon's world. It took a lot to surprise him. Having a right-wing activist sitting across the desk from him would be ranked up there with top-notch bombshells to drop into his lap.

Julian Marshal, the leader for the extremist group The Purity of Humanity, had come knocking just over an hour ago. The Purity of Humanity had been around for a few years, trying to remove the rights of the irregulars. The group claimed that rights were for living, breathing humans and not animals or Hellyon. Animals didn't vote. Why should it matter how many legs they walked on? Vampyres were legally dead. Those who were smart enough to stay buried didn't have the right to vote, so why should the bloodsuckers? More than their storefront, The Purity nutcases took out who they could when no one was looking.

"What can I do for you, Mr. Marshal?" Deagon asked, checking his watch.

He had about fifteen minutes before he had to prepare his next shipment. His Calyph would be arriving to do the grunt labor and transport the product. Those who had lived in the trenches knew the game and could play it blindfolded. He had no further use for outside help, not when he had men who knew the business better than anyone he could hire in.

"Your club will be raided at midnight. A warrant was signed a couple of hours ago." Julian said, pushing an envelope across Deagon's black desk. "We keep an eye on what warrants are signed and who The Netherworld is looking at. It's in our best interest to know what's going down in our city."

Deagon grabbed the envelope then pulled out a copy of the warrant and a few photos. Captain Salas Warner — Des' old boss — was standing in front of The Netherworld HQ, talking to a few suits, holding what appeared to be a folded-up warrant. Deagon flipped to the warrant. They were looking for drugs and weapons, both of which Deagon was fully stocked with. His walls were pretty much painted in blow and gunpowder.

"Where did you get this and how much is this intel gonna cost me?" Deagon asked, glancing up from a handful of reasons he'd be in jail before the sun came up.

"Like I said, it's in our best interest to know what's going down in our city. One never knows what information will come in handy," Julian answered. He moved closer to the desk and lowered his voice as if he feared being overheard. "I have a few men with me here tonight. We can help you move out your product to a safe location. In turn, we are in need of a man like you."

Deagon leaned back in his chair, looking at his watch again. The warrant would be executed in just over an hour. He couldn't move the product without being caught. The feds were probably circling the wagons as they spoke.

"How the hell are you going to walk out with my load?"

"We won't get all of it, but whatever we can't move, I've got it covered," Julian said, sounding sure of himself.

"What exactly do you need with me?" Deagon asked, curious.

"You may have heard that our spokesman was taken out by a Vamp a few weeks back. We've been following you for some time. We both know you need the front and we need someone who isn't afraid to get dirty."

Deagon nodded. It did have a nice ring to it. Julian was right. It would give him the front he needed and an endless supply of men he could pick from, for the Order. And at this point, he didn't have much of a choice. He was over a barrel but wasn't about to show it.

"I'm in, on my terms, which we will discuss at a later date," Deagon said, standing up. "Let's get this show on the road, shall we?"

Julian stood, smiling ear to ear. "Point me in the direction of your product. Let your men know to stand down, and we'll take care of the rest. Stay in your office. Get rid of anything that'll land you in an orange jumpsuit and a stint with The Netherworld. Let me and my men handle the particulars."

Deagon called Prudence into his office, passed on the word then watched her walk out of the door with Julian. He took what little blow he had in his office and flushed it down the drain. He burned the bills he'd used to suck the shit up his nose and dumped the ashes with the powder he loved more than his beating heart.

He poured a drink, thankful he was actually sober for once. He watched the monitors from his black leather chair. Nothing looked out of the ordinary in his club, no commotion that stood out. But Deagon could see Julian moving through the crowd, getting his men together. Splitting up, twenty young men and women each pocketed what they could and made their way to the door. All of them were cheering and making a scene, staggering and raving about another club up the road. They were celebrating a wedding — or that was what it looked like. He remembered their reservations. The party had been here for almost two hours. *Sneaky little twerp, that Julian was*, Deagon thought to himself with a grin.

Deagon watched most of his product make its way out the door. But that left the weapons. Deagon watched Julian pass a long black duffle bag to a man who looked like he'd spent a few solid years behind bars and had the matching tattoos to boot. The man took the bag then a seat in the back. Another man took a seat across from him, holding a thick manila envelope, both looking like a deal was going down.

Deagon was impressed. Julian had brought his own fall guys in, to take a rap that would have sent Deagon to prison. He'd thought this one through. Clearly they wanted Deagon badly enough to send two of their own to prison. This was either going to be really good for him or really fucking bad.

At exactly midnight, the doors to the club were streaming with The Netherworld. Cops, feds and agents poured into Deagon's club, shutting down the party. The music came to a halt and his office door crashed open.

Deagon, sitting at his desk, paperwork spread out in front of him, looked up. He feigned a look of surprise as his office filled with badges. Captain Salas Warner stepped in, holding a warrant and a smug look on his face.

"Can I help you?" Deagon asked, standing up.

"We have a warrant to search the premises of The Hemlock, Mr. Jackston."

Deagon stepped from around his desk, grabbed the warrant and read it as if he hadn't just seen it an hour before. And true to Julian's word, they were here for drugs and weapons. Deagon stepped aside and let them go to work.

"Go right ahead, Officer," Deagon said and moved out of his office.

His club was crawling with agents. From the front of the club, Julian came walking.

"Mr. Jackston, sorry it took so long to get here. Your club manager called me," Julian said, stepping around Deagon, extending his hand to Captain Warner. "Good evening, I'm Mr. Jackston's attorney, Julian Marshal. May I view the warrant?"

Warner glared but handed it over. Julian skimmed through it then nodded. "Keep in mind, gentlemen... If you break it, you bought it. Come on, Mr. Jackston. Let's grab a drink and let these fine gentlemen do their jobs."

Deagon followed Julian to a table off the dance floor and watched as his club was ripped apart. Thirty minutes into the search and the two men who had been holding the guns were found.

When questioned, Julian wouldn't allow Deagon to

answer, stating Deagon would be firing his door security and making adjustments to policy. He could not be held responsible for the actions of two strangers. Deagon thanked the officers for getting the guns off the streets, stating they would be issuing a press release, commending the fine work of the local police.

To most of them, Deagon was a retired cop. So far it appeared like the captain was the only one with the knowledge of who Deagon really was. Clearly that bit of intel was under wraps at the moment. The development of the Slayers was still underground and he knew that Warner couldn't say a word about secret ops. It didn't stop him from giving Deagon the evil eye, though.

The search came and went. Somehow the security tapes for the night had malfunctioned, so no gold could be found there. Nothing could be pinned on Deagon. They'd investigate the arms dealing going down in the club, but Julian assured Deagon that the two men would roll over and take a deal, never naming Deagon. In turn, The Purity of Humanity would be coughing up some serious cash for their families.

Julian and Deagon parted ways, with the agreement that Deagon would help Julian bring the irregulars down. It was a win-win for Deagon. He hated the irregulars as much as Julian and his people did.

Deagon took a seat and kicked his feet up. Slowly and steadily, he would take down the Slayers, from the top. A whole new world of opportunity had come knocking and Deagon had opened the door happily. Life was good.

Chapter Thirteen

Cael and Des had paced the hallway for hours, waiting for Sid to return from the Orygin. Each noise had brought their heads around the corner. The moment Sid arrived back at the compound, Des and Cael cried, grabbing Sid and bringing him to his bedroom. Riam had watched Cael, realizing what he'd said was true. Cael loved Sid as he loved Des, completely. Riam hadn't noticed it before. He'd felt uncomfortable with love and discussing relationships, but, in that moment, he hadn't needed words to understand where Cael was coming from.

Sasha had been unconscious for two days. Each time she'd stirred, Neri had upped the meds. Her body was in rough shape. Opal had stuck around to mend the worst of the injuries — broken bones, internal bleeding and any mark that would leave a scar. She didn't want Sasha to have the constant reminder of her hellish journey when she looked in the mirror. Opal had left one scar on Sasha's lower back, as a reminder of fighting her way through hell and surviving. It was the way of the Seers, to always carry a reminder of what they were fighting for. For some, they held tokens from their families. For others, it was a scar or a tattoo.

Riam had sat beside her bed, reading to her. Neri had said his voice kept her calm and whenever he was out of the room, she would begin to stir. Rather than keeping her hopped up on the juice and having her developing a dependency, Riam had read to her.

At first, he'd felt odd, out of place. This wasn't him. He wasn't the man who sat beside a woman's bed, reading. He wasn't the type to listen to someone's heartbeat, counting the beats per minute. But there he was, on the floor, leaning against the bed, reading Oscar Fingal O'Flahertie Wills Wilde, better known as simply Oscar Wilde.

Riam had met the Irish writer in London in the late eighteen-hundreds. Sitting in a pub, they'd traded stories. Riam's bookshelves were lined with his works, along with another Irish writer, James Joyce, and Russian writer Fyodor Mikhailovich Dostoyevsky. He'd favored Ernest Hemmingway and William Cuthbert Faulkner and had almost every print they had penned. Reading had been Riam's only solitude, his escape from a world that beat him down each time he stepped outside.

Captain Salas Warner had called Cael with an update of the raid on The Hemlock. Warner had mentioned Deagon's new lawyer, Julian Marshal. Everyone knew who he was—a slimy lawyer who was balls deep in The Purity of Humanity, a half-crazed group of idiots who thought the world would be a better place if only one race existed. Sounded a lot like the first speech Hitler gave, before he tried to cleanse the world.

The raid hadn't turned up anything more than two arms dealers, neither of whom could be connected to Deagon or his shitbucket of a lawyer. The place was clean. They had suspected sex trade but couldn't prove it. No one was talking and no evidence had turned up. Riam's intel on who owned the club had left them no further ahead. The Netherworld would be keeping an eye on the club, but Warner wasn't hopeful.

The Slayers surrounded the long table in the meeting room, going over the newest intel from Warner, when Neri busted into the room, putting her arms up in the frame of the doorway, blocking the path.

"Get the fuck out of my way, little lady, before I remove your fucking arms." Sasha's voice vibrated into the room and grabbed Riam's attention by the balls.

Riam turned to see Sasha standing a few feet from Neri, wearing hospital scrubs and holding a scalpel out in front of her body. She held the little surgical knife as if it were her last chance, gripped in her white-knuckled fist and ready to throw down.

"No. Drop the knife or I will use it to cut your throat, old woman," Neri replied, standing her ground.

Riam looked to Zylan, who didn't move from the table. He stood grinning at the spectacle. Zylan had learned not to rescue Neri. She didn't like it. Zylan would swoop in if he thought Neri couldn't handle it on her own. Seeing him stand there made the rest of the Slayers turn to watch but not act on it. Riam knew Neri was a ball of fire and would throw down regardless of winning or losing. She was just that stubborn.

"Do you have any idea who you're fucking with?" Sasha asked.

Neri laughed, throwing her head back in a dramatic display. "Do you have any idea who *you* are fucking with? Drop the scalpel and maybe, just maybe, I'll let you pass. You're not taking my equipment in there. They'll break my stuff. Do you know how hard it is for me to leave to replace it? I don't have time for this shit. Drop it or I take it out of your dead fucking fingers."

"Wait. You're worried about your little scalpel and not me cutting them?"

Neri laughed again. "Oh, hell no. I just want my equipment back. Drop it and do what you want. They can handle themselves. That scalpel means nothing to them, but it means something to me. Last warning, then I'm going to go apeshit."

Sasha laughed. The sound carried into the room and twitched the wicked creature in his pants to life. Riam's eyes widened. He felt the heat rise to his cheeks. Was he blushing? He didn't blush.

Neri put her arms down and wiggled them lose. She got into position, turning her body sideways. Riam watched her take a deep, cleansing breath, in through her nose and out of her mouth. She rolled her shoulders and brought her

107

hands up into tight fists.

"I warned you, Sasha," Neri said calmly.

Sasha grinned and dropped the scalpel. Neri didn't budge.

"My money is on Neri. She broke my nose in training a week ago," Sid said, dropping twenty bucks on the table.

Bane dropped a twenty on the table. "I'm in. I'm with Sid. My money is on the Dr. Frankenstein. Crazy bitch kicked me in the head while I was sleeping, payback for touching her medical supplies without filling out her stupid log book."

"It's not stupid, wolf. I need to know what's being taken so we always have what we need," Neri called back to Bane. "Bitch and whine some more and the next time you need me to stitch you up, I'll make you fill out requisition forms in triplicate."

Sasha rolled her shoulders and gave Neri a bow then moved into a karate pose.

Neri nodded, returning the bow. "I am a tenth dan, red belt in karate. My grandfather was my mother's village grandmaster."

Riam watched Neri and Sasha square off. Sasha was good but blinded by her need to win. Her hunger for hate kept her one step behind Neri. Neri fought with liquid grace — calm, cool and collected. Her movements were elegant, yet powerful. Her feet slid across the wooden floor, each step thought out before it landed. Every hit had a purpose. While Sasha fought with a greed for the win, Neri fought to protect herself.

When Sasha was down and almost out, Neri stepped back. Neri had honor. Sasha did not. When Neri's back was turned, Sasha tried to attack. But Neri was no fool. She knew the Seer would expose her gutlessness. Neri turned at the last moment and sucker-punched Sasha in her jaw. Sasha went down with Neri riding her body to the floor.

Neri scooped up her scalpel and brought it to Sasha's throat. "Enough. I am *not* your enemy, and I will not be your next victim."

Sasha leaned her head back. "Do it. I know you want to. Just do it."

Neri leaned into Sasha's face, making eye contact. "You are not the only one who has lived through hell. You are not the only one within these walls who has had their world smashed into pieces in front of their eyes. Crawl out of your wounds. You bring disgrace to their memory. You bring no righteousness to your fight by choosing a path that would dishonor your family. Do not shame yourself like this. They would not want this."

Sasha rolled her head to the side, leaning on the blade. "Please, end it. I'm begging you. End me."

Neri climbed off of Sasha. "One day, Sasha, you will understand why I didn't take your life. I am not a murderer. I would never dishonor my family in that way."

Zylan finally moved from the table, taking the money bet against Neri off the table. "I'm taking this as a lesson. That's what you get for gambling, suckers."

He helped Neri off the floor, picking up the scalpel then handing it to her.

"You fought well, young grasshopper." Zylan grinned, kissing her nose.

"If my scalpel has even one tiny scratch, I'm going postal," Neri said, tucking her head into her Fyrvor, yawning.

Riam knelt beside Sasha, lifting her up and into his arms. "I should have warned you, Neri is particular about her clinic."

Sasha glanced up, blushing, with tears in her eyes. "I can see that."

"She's kicked all of our asses, including mine. My sight doesn't work with her. She moves too quickly and changes it up before my sight can catch up. With her, the only thing that works is skill," Riam said, helping Sasha stand.

"Well, this was bloody embarrassing," Sasha whispered, looking around Riam's body at the Slayers.

Riam shrugged. "Don't worry about it. This place is a

madhouse. You should have seen Neri beat the crap out of Sidriel. He ran through the house screaming like a girl with Neri on his back, trying to choke him out."

"I wasn't screaming like a girl. She has tiny arms and was pinching my vocal cords. My voice came out a little higher. That's all," Sid called from the table. "I could have taken her down. I just don't hit girls."

"Right. That's why you ran, screaming for help?" Bane joked, laughing.

Riam led Sasha to the table, where she apologized. Riam could see the anger still floating under the surface of her skin, like heat waves on hot pavement. It felt like he was standing too close to a bonfire. She may have looked calm, but Riam knew she was housing enough anger to burn them all.

"I was so close to him." Sasha started talking. "If you would have given me another day or two in there, I could have killed him. I know it."

Opal, who had been standing in the corner, stepped forward. "Sasha, you would have died. Maybe in another minute, or hour or day. I'm not sure when, but I am certain that you were soon to die from infection. Do you remember why you were there?"

Sasha frowned. "He took me when the warehouse went down."

"Yes, but do you know why?" Opal asked again.

"Torture? Hate? Because he could? Why else does that shit happen?" Sasha asked, glaring.

"To procreate with you. As you know, he can only create life with a Seer. He took you in order to create another Strain," Opal answered. "Soon, he would have planted his seed in your womb and all hope would have been lost."

Bellum chose that time to step into the room, holding her hands up and moving to the farthest end of the table from Sasha.

Sasha stared at Bellum for a moment, her brain figuring out who she was. Sasha looked to Riam then back to Bellum.

"You're working with the Strains, with the Genesys?"

"No, it's not like that, Sasha." Riam tried to explain.

Sasha ducked under Riam's arm and lunged for Bellum.

"Let her come," Bellum called out and the table cleared.

As Sasha touched Bellum, Riam's hand was still holding on to her. Bellum unleashed her memories, flooding Sasha and Riam with her entire history. Bellum had worked against her father from the moment of maturity until now. She had hidden Seers from him, placing the stones from the darkness inside their bodies while they slept. She had rescued those her father had taken, leaving no trace of them behind. Those she had killed were people who would willingly follow her father.

Every night, Bellum had prayed to the Orygin for strength. She had begged for her life and to remain strong enough to save humanity. She had punished herself when she stepped off her righteous path and had hated herself for who she was.

The night Sasha's home had been destroyed, Bellum had been there. She had risked her life inside the home, trying to get to Sasha's children before the explosion. She had fhaded into the home as the blast took down the house. She'd tried to take them but had been too late. She had gotten Sasha's family out before the house burned to a crisp and had bargained with destiny to allow them to go to Elysium. She had given fate her own ability to have children, her ability to love another, to buy their existence and send them to the Orygin. Bellum had waited with a dagger in her hand for a Journeyer to take Sasha's family home.

Bellum had sworn, in that very moment, to rise up and fight against the evil that had plagued the world. She had spent every day hunting evil from that moment on. Taking out the wicked and saving those who were innocent. She had done it knowing she could be discovered and taken back to the darkness. But it was the night she'd spent protecting Sasha's family, hearing Sasha's cries carried in the wind, that had been the turning point for Bellum. It had been enough to push her to do everything in her power to keep that sadness from another doorstep.

Bellum pulled back, staring into Sasha's eyes. "You cannot alter the future without punishment. But that didn't mean you should have suffered as you did. I'm sorry for your loss. I'm sorry that my family played a part in it. I wish I could have saved them. I have tried to protect your people, but I have failed."

Sasha staggered backward. Riam held her standing.

"Thank you," Sasha whispered. "You did save them. In the end, you saved the parts of them I valued most, their souls. I wanted a life. I wanted love, so I forced it to happen. It was so real. I knew what would happen, but I thought I could protect them. I thought that destiny would give me a break, for all the good I had done. But it didn't care. It took back what I had stolen and the pain blinded me."

"It blinds us all," Bellum agreed.

"It hurts, so badly, that some days I can't breathe or think. I just want it to end, but I won't kill myself or I'll never see them again. I'll go to Hades."

Riam lifted Sasha into his arms and carried her from the meeting room. He pushed open the door to his bedroom, carrying her inside. They were running low on sleeping quarters and he had no other option aside from the clinic. He wasn't about to tuck her into a hospital bed. He set her on his feather bed and pulled the blankets over her. He grabbed another book off his shelf and sat on the floor, reading to her.

"I could hear you reading to me," Sasha whispered, curling onto her side to face Riam.

Riam looked up from his book. "It seemed to keep you calm."

"I miss them, Riam. It kills me. Every day I die all over again from the pain of losing them."

Riam closed his book and turned to face her. "I've never lost a child or a partner. I cannot imagine your pain. But I know life goes on, with or without you. That's how the world works. It doesn't care about your pain. The world keeps moving forward. Living in your wounds only keeps them wide open. The pain will always be there. It dulls over time, but the wound on your soul will never truly heal because part of it is gone. Eventually, the sadness becomes part of the memory, and you learn to move on."

"I don't want to move on," Sasha whispered, squeezing her eyes closed.

Riam reached for her hand and he let her grip it. "If you had perished, would you not wish for your partner to live? To love again? To become whole again? What if you were looking down on him, day in and day out, watching him slowly die of loneliness and hate? Would you want this for him? Or for your children?"

Sasha shook her head. "That's different."

"No, it isn't. You need to say goodbye. You need to let them go, let them move on to their next lives."

Sasha pulled her eyes open, frowning. "What do you mean, move on to their next lives? They're already gone."

Riam nodded. "But you also know what Seers believe. Holding on to your loved ones too tightly could keep them here, stuck in the in-between. It is why we hold our ceremonies and we meditate. We say our goodbyes and we wish them Godspeed to Elysium. Did you hold a death ceremony?"

Sasha shook her head. "I couldn't do it. I couldn't say goodbye."

"Have you tried speaking to your partner? I speak to my sister, Layla, each time I meditate. It gives me strength."

"Does she ever answer back?"

Riam smiled. "Not with words, but I can feel her. I feel her in my soul. I feel her each time I leave for a hunt. She will always be with me."

"I can't feel them, Riam. I didn't get to say goodbye. I didn't get to tell them how much I love them," Sasha cried. Tears flowed from her eyes and soaked into the pillow.

Riam could taste the saltiness of the sadness in the air.

"They know, Sasha. They already know how much you love them."

Riam sat with Sasha for hours, letting her talk about her family in a way that wasn't tragically wounding. They both laughed and both cried. It was the purest moment Riam had experienced in too many years to count. Sasha's soul was still stuck in the moment she'd realized she had lost them. It was still sitting on the pavement her body had landed on, her home and life in shambles in front of her. It had not moved beyond that very first twinge of pain. Riam held her as she cried, truly mourning her loss.

As the sun began to rise, Riam walked with her in the field behind the compound, finding the perfect spot to see the sun come up over the mountains. Kneeling with Sasha and spreading a ring of salt, they meditated. Sasha gripped his hand as she reached out with her heart and soul to finally say goodbye. Riam had never felt more honored than that moment, to share such a personal and painful experience with someone.

The wind picked up her hair and twisted it around her body, cleaning the tears from her cheeks. Riam watched as her shoulders straightened and her head lifted. She finally opened her puffy eyes, and she breathed her first clean breath since the last one she'd taken inside her old home.

The road to her mending would be a long one, and Opal had agreed to return weekly, to help Sasha meditate and cleanse her soul of hate and sadness. Sasha would remain with the Slayers. She wouldn't take no for an answer. She wanted to fight against the evil. She wouldn't allow her heartache to take hold of another family.

Cael and Des had thought the idea would blow up in their faces, Sid didn't have an opinion and Bane wasn't asked because he'd agree with Riam. Zylan would side with Neri. Which meant the deciding vote came down to Neri. Sasha was ready to pack her bags, thinking Neri didn't like her, when Neri welcomed Sasha aboard.

"Touch my stuff and I'll break your fingers. Got it?" Neri

asked.

Sasha nodded her head, lips pursed, trying not to cry. "Thank you," she choked out.

"Welcome to our little shit show," Neri said and gave her a hug.

"Once you're in, you're all the way in. Toe-tagged is your only way out," Cael said then gave Riam a long stare. "No more of this cowboy rodeo bullshit. My heart can't take this crap."

Sasha would remain in Riam's bedroom, and Riam would take over the living room, which sounded brilliant until the first night sleeping in there.

"Can you believe this shit?" Zylan shouted out to Sid, as they watched an old Vampyre movie. "Since when do we stop to count grains of rice?"

"Simmer down, fang face, and just watch the fuckin' show," Sid called back from a recliner chair.

"What's up with no reflections or not being able to cross moving water? This movie is lame."

Riam opened his eyes and looked at Zy. "Hey 'tard, this is based on the lies our people have told. It was so that we could pass their tests. If we could see our reflection in a mirror or swim across a stream, we were less likely to be stabbed through the heart. It is the same for Therians, or Lycans — whatever the movies are calling them. They were tied to a tree on a full moon to see if they'd shift. The folklore says that a man cannot control his beast. When they didn't shift, they were freed. More lies told to keep our kind safe."

"Wait, Therians aren't controlled by the moon?" Zylan asked, frowning.

Bane jumped over the back of the couch, not realizing Riam was sleeping there, landing on his stomach. "Nope. The younger ones are, but it's because of the energy in the air that the full moon brings. Stick them in the middle of a rave, at noon, and they'd shift there too."

Riam sat up, groaning and shoving Bane off him. "Each one of you fuckers has a television in their bedroom. Why the hell must you be out here?"

"I'm scared of the dark," Sid joked.

Sasha took a seat on the couch next to Riam. "You don't know darkness until you've been where I've been."

Sid blushed. "I didn't mean..."

Sasha winked. "I was once stuck inside of a whale. It took two hours to get out. Well, I had dropped a few hits of E and thought I was stuck inside of a whale. Turns out, I was wrapped up in a sleeping bag. But just the same, it was dark as hell. Woodstock really kicked my ass."

The rest of the hours melted by. Soon, all of the Slayers had found their way into the living room with beers and snacks. They had joked and told stories of embarrassment and stories of victory. Riam watched each of them in a way he never had before. Usually, he would leave when everyone gathered together. But this time, he'd stayed and laughed with them. Riam had finally fallen asleep, leaning against the wall with Sasha's head on his lap and his arm draped across her shoulders.

It had felt right, having her near him. He wouldn't push her or mention his feelings, but he would make sure she knew there was someone in this world that cared for her.

Chapter Fourteen

Deagon stood at a podium in front of over three hundred people, media included. The Purity of Humanity had rented the Art Gallery for a little meet and greet. Halfway through the evening, following dinner, it was Deagon's turn to address the guests. Julian had written a speech for Deagon, which he'd read and rolled his eyes at. Making a few last minute changes to the pep talk, Deagon took his place at the front of the room.

"Ladies and gentlemen, I thank you for coming out tonight. As I know you are all very busy out there in a world overrun by…" Deagon looked at his notes, lifted the little white cards and ripped them for all to see. Julian's face paled.

Deagon stepped out from behind the podium and unbuttoned his suit jacket. He pulled it off and tossed it to the chairs beside him. He rolled up his sleeves then put his hands on his hips.

"Mr. Marshal spent many hours writing a speech that would knock your socks off. For that, I'm grateful. Hours upon hours of time, he slaves away for this organization and asks for no credit. He truly is the man behind all of this," Deagon said, motioning toward Julian. "As for myself, I'm like you all. I work. I pay my taxes. I take transit and I pick up the trash in my neighborhood. I put on my pants, one leg at a time, and fight my way through life. Just this morning I asked myself if I wanted to eat tonight or if I wanted to pay my power bill. I'm no one special. I'm no more important than the man outside parking the cars. I'm of no more value than the prostitute a few of you will be picking up on your way home."

Deagon winked and chuckled. A few men chimed in with him. Deagon kept his bullshit going, one lie after the next.

"Let me get to the point of tonight. I used to be a cop. I thought I could take out the bad guys with a badge. Only I learned that the organization I worked for was dirtier than the scum I was trying to lock up. I used to be a lot of things, one of which was not hungry. I used to be able to put food on my table without risking running water and electricity. I used to want children. Now I'm so afraid of the future I would be handing over that I won't. I won't have a family because I'm too scared I won't be able to protect them against something that wants their blood or a man not being able to control his wolf so it cuts loose in a school playground."

The audience murmured, agreeing with his fears. Sure, Deagon knew his words were a load of trumped-up lies, but they were eating it up. Fear bred stupidity.

"I'm not saying irregulars should die. I would never endorse genocide. That is not the answer and anyone who thinks that way needs to walk out those doors," Deagon said, pointing to the rear of the room. "I won't be a part of it and you won't be a part of this."

The room fell silent, and Julian managed to grow white enough to appear sickly. But Deagon knew that no one in here would risk publicly signing up for mass murder, especially not with the media present.

With a nod, Deagon continued. "We will not lower ourselves to monsters. We simply ask our leaders to review the law and uphold it. Irregulars were never made true, legal citizens. We simply ask that be upheld. If my dog attacked my neighbor, I would put it down without a second thought. And I wouldn't face criminal charges for it either. My goldfish doesn't vote. Why? Because it is not a human being, with the rights and liberties of mankind. We wish for law and order. We want our children to be safe. We want to be able to walk home at night and not fear our pulse can be heard by a blood drinker. We want what we were promised, what our men and women have died for, our basic rights and freedoms." Deagon pointed at an elderly man in the audience. "You, sir... Did you fight in our wars for this?"

The man shook his head. "No, sir. I fought for freedom."

"Do you feel free? Do you feel your children and their children are safe to walk home at night?"

"Hell no, I don't. My granddaughter was attacked by a Vamp, just five weeks ago," the elderly man answered.

Deagon knew the man had been planted there by Julian. It was to be part of the act tonight.

"I thank you, personally, for your sacrifice, sir," Deagon said, then brought his hand to his forehead and gave him a salute. Deagon went back to the group. "We need your help to get this ball rolling. Those who cannot afford to help, we still thank you and appreciate you being here and hearing our plea to our leaders. Those who can spare a few bucks, know this. Every nickel we get goes into every inch we gain in this war against humanity. Thank you. Thank you all for your support. And thank you to Julian for the meal. Looks like I get to pay my power bill, as he's been gracious enough to allow me to take leftovers home."

As Deagon stepped off the stage, a woman dripping in diamonds and old money stopped him in his tracks. She slid a check into his hand.

"This should help you eat for a few months, Deagon. Bless your heart," she said, with tears forming in her eyes.

Deagon gave her a fake smile. "I cannot personally take your money, ma'am. I was taught to work for my keep."

Her face all but melted off the bone in sympathy. "Don't be foolish. I have more money than I know what to do with and not once did I work for it. Feed yourself and make an old woman happy."

Deagon eyed the check—fifty thousand, for twenty minutes of work. "Thank you. Bless your sweetness. You will forever be in my prayers."

Deagon stopped every three or four feet, collecting more money. Julian moved around the room, grabbing his fair share of cash. Ending the night with almost a half mil wasn't a bad start to the job. Deagon dumped the cash on Julian and was out of the back door.

Julian made true on his word. The drugs had made it out the other side and the weapons had gone missing from the evidence locker, finding their way back to Deagon. He had a new shipment coming in and had to beat street to make it in time. Although he trusted his new Calyph more than any other he'd had, he still liked being there when his product arrived.

Since the night of the Netherworld raid on his club, he'd started weaning himself off the blow. Had he been balls to the wall high during the raid, he'd have been fucked. Now that he was climbing back out from under his father, he didn't need that shit anymore. He needed a clear mind, a level head, and he had to be able to string together more than three coherent words.

It didn't stop Deagon from making one pit stop. He was all fired up and needed to get out a little hate before hitting the warehouse. The evil inside Deagon needed an exit or he'd be back on the smack before he could think twice.

"Fifty for a suck and a hundred for a full ride," the whore called out from the bathroom at The Hemlock.

Deagon pushed open the door to find his usual kneeling on the floor, paper towels from the holder piled under her bruised knees. Her hair was tangled and her eyeliner was dripping down her cheeks. She was a hot mess, leaning more toward mess.

"Tsk, tsk, Ronnie. You know you're not allowed to do business in my club," Deagon said, shutting the door behind him. "What did I say would happen if I caught you selling your ass in here?"

Ronnie's brown eyes widened. "I'm sorry, Deagon."

Deagon knew she would be there. She strolled in every time she watched him leave. Deagon had been counting on her being around. He loved a good struggle fuck and an angry pounding.

Ronnie tried to stand, but Deagon pushed her shoulders back down. "Where do you think you're going?"

Ronnie rolled her eyes up, glaring. "Nowhere."

"If you want to fuck in my club, you're going to pay rent," Deagon said, glaring back.

He unzipped his black dress pants and pulled her face toward him. Her hair was sticky with hairspray and other things he didn't want to even think of. Feeling her hot mouth wrap around him made his shoulders relax and his grin widen.

"That's right. Earn it." Deagon moaned, pumping his hips into her mouth.

He closed his eyes and thought of Desdemona, his lust for her and his hate. His need to have her again was filled with his disgust for wanting her. He looked down at the whore on her knees and he could almost picture Des.

"Des," Deagon whispered.

He lifted Ronnie off her knees and turned her around. He leaned her over the white porcelain sink to take her from behind. He hated having to look a whore in the eyes. It killed the moment for him. He held her by the back of the hair and sunk his cock into her greedy body. Every slap of his hips on her ass made him hate her just a little more. He wrapped his hands around her throat and squeezed. The whore panicked, clawing at them. Deagon pounded against her harder until his balls seized and he dumped himself inside her.

She dropped to her knees, gasping for air while Deagon cleaned himself off in the sink. "Next time, I'd advise you to think very hard about whether you are willing to pay rent here again."

"Bastard." She choked on the word.

Deagon grinned. "Indeed, I am. Run along now, before there is interest tacked on."

Ronnie scrambled off of the floor and out the door.

Pleased with himself, he hit the road. He watched Prudence give Ronnie a fistful of cash to shut her up, telling her not to come back. Deagon gave Prudence a wave and walked out of the front door with a bounce in his step.

Chapter Fifteen

Two months had passed for Sasha since the moment of her rescue. Each day had been its own brutal journey. But little by little it got easier. The nights were the most difficult, closing her eyes and being completely alone. Saying goodbye to her family had given her soul freedom and permission to heal, but it had also removed her crutch. It had removed her reason to get out of bed and to breathe.

Time with Opal had reminded her of every reason she had to get up in the morning, why she was important and that even in the darkest of hours, she was loved. They had meditated together weekly, calming her soul and centering her thoughts. She would become a Slayer, fighting only a righteous fight. It would take discipline to keep her from returning to her darker side, but she was willing to keep her torch burning, lighting her way.

Every evening, without fail, Riam would take her for a walk. He would listen to her struggles and her memories. He would challenge her thoughts and correct her hate. He was more than a friend. She knew he loved her in his own way, but never once did he force his feelings or touch her in a way that would make her feel like she was dishonoring Henry, her fallen partner. Simply put, Riam had become her anchor, keeping her from venturing too far out into the cold alone.

The part of her heart that had said she would never love again had thawed. Through meditation and pure honesty, she knew Henry would want her to move on. He would want her to love again, to be happy and to have the life he had planned for them to have together. She knew she would want the same for him.

Sitting cross-legged, facing each other, Sasha and Riam meditated. With the trees surrounding them, opening up above at a clear night, Sasha felt calmer than she ever had. The wind touched her face, bringing smells of life into her body.

"I love you too, Riam," Sasha whispered, opening her eyes to see his shocked expression. "I can feel your love, and I thank you for bringing me back, for lighting the way and holding my hand as I healed. You have been my Aegys, from the moment you saw me trapped behind that door. I knew you'd come for me. Even when I had lost hope, my soul still hung on to the knowledge that one day, you'd pull me from that pit and my own darkness."

Sasha's words echoed in Riam's ears. At first, he thought he'd wished for it, to the point where he was imagining how it would sound. When he opened his eyes to see Sasha's mouth moving, he knew it was real. He knew she was speaking the words his heart had craved since the moment of his birthing.

"Crap, Riam. Are you okay?" Sasha asked, getting onto her knees and leaning in to Riam.

He frowned for a moment. "Of course I'm okay. I'm more than okay."

"You're crying," Sasha whispered, pulling a tear from his cheek for him to see. "I thought I said something wrong."

Riam hadn't realized his eyes had sprung a leak. He smiled and shook his head. "I'm very okay, Sasha. I've waited my entire life for someone to love me. I didn't think I was deserving of such things."

Riam felt her warm lips press against his, she whispered into his mouth between the kisses. "You are a better man than you think you are, Riam. I love you."

Riam's shoulders shook with relief. His body trembled as his soul finally stretched from behind its wall of safety. He was finally loved by a woman he would die for.

Pulling her face toward him gently, he kissed her back. He drank down her love and let it warm him to the core.

"My Fyrvor," Riam said. The moment he spoke the words, the instinct to take her to the ground and mount her filled his veins. His hips jerked toward her as his cock woke to the news of having a woman at his side. He shook his head and pulled back, blushing. "Sorry, I'm...shit...sorry."

Sasha crawled onto his lap and wrapped her legs around his waist. "The drive for our kind to bed their mate is one of our most basic and strongest instincts, Riam. Do not apologize for your biology."

Riam breathed in her scent and groaned with need. Had he been full Vampyre, he'd have sunk his teeth into her neck at that very moment. The passion between two Seers could be overwhelming. Their inner lights called to each other, like two leviathans in the deep.

"I don't want to rush you," Riam said, after pulling his mouth from hers but still holding her face in his hands.

Sasha kissed the tip of his nose. "I trust you. My soul trusts you. You would never rush or hurt me."

"I'd die before I harmed a hair on your head," Riam said, looking her in the eyes.

Sasha grabbed a fistful of his hair and pulled it back, exposing his throat. "Sometimes a gal likes it rough."

Riam's hips reared up the moment Sasha bit into his flesh. She wasn't a full Vampyre either, not yet. But the feeling of her teeth on his throat had sent his mind screaming and every drop of blood it could into the head of his cock.

He spun them around with Sasha's back on the ground and Riam on top. "I have to taste you, please. I need to swallow you down."

Sasha grinned and nodded. She didn't have the chance to help Riam pull her clothes off. Riam had torn her black leggings from her body, snapping the sides of her thong. Her legs were open and resting on either side of his head before she had her shirt off.

Riam brought his hand up to her chest and pushed her

upper body to the ground, making her squirm. His teeth nipped at her inner thigh as he breathed her into his lungs. He almost lost it. His cock strained against his pants and hammered into the earth. He pushed himself harder into the ground, keeping pressure on himself or he was likely to come in his pants.

Riam explored every inch of her, lapping at her delicate juices as though he were starved. He couldn't get enough of her. He needed more. He built her orgasm, knowing it was literally on the tip of his tongue. With her groaning into the night, he pushed a finger inside her and pulled her button into his mouth, working her feverishly.

The forest came alive with her scream. It echoed through the trees and bounced back, hitting Riam in the center of his brain. He had never worked for something so hard as he had the moment his mouth filled with her pleasure. He was driven to bring it to her again. It was more important than his next breath.

Sasha grabbed his head and ground her hips against his face, panting his name, calling out for more. He was more than happy to oblige. Hell, had she asked for his heart, he'd have carved that out for her too.

Riam was off in his own world of 'is this a dream', so Sasha pushed at him with her feet, rolling him over on his back. Sasha didn't waste any time. She climbed onto him, sitting her button back on his tongue and riding him from above, her body facing backward to view his vibrating hips. Riam was back in heaven, working her into a moaning frenzy. His hips jerked as she pulled his belt off and unzipped his pants. Before he could tell her that it wasn't necessary, that he was content with giving her pleasure, her mouth engulfed his rock-hard need. Riam growled into her body, his hips dancing to a beat of their own.

"When I go, you go," Sasha said as she lifted off for a moment then took him deeply and sucked Riam's shaft.

He wanted to save it and mark her body with it. But he didn't push his luck. Her hips rocked against his tongue and her moans covered his hips. Her paced quickened. He knew she was close and he was thankful for it. He didn't know how much longer he could hold out. Her mouth was so unbelievably warm, with each pump and lick of her tongue, she would follow it up with her hands stroking him or cupping his balls.

"Close," she groaned, rocking faster on his tongue.

Riam reached between their bodies, finding her nipples and giving them a slight pinch. That was exactly what she needed to send her over the edge. He held on to them, adding more pressure with each one of her moans. Her body vibrated and she screamed around his cock, drinking it down.

Riam's orgasm had been building for several minutes, and with hers raining down on his tongue, he couldn't hold back any longer. His hips jumped to meet her mouth. He groaned into her body as his seed flowed into her throat.

"Fuck," Riam gasped, his hips still twitching and dancing.

Sasha kept the pace until he was spent and every drop of him that could possibly escape had been drunk down. Riam hadn't stopped licking at her pleasure. He went on until she settled and pulled away.

"Wow," Sasha whispered, with a shaky voice.

She plunked down beside him, resting her head on his arm. He could hear her heart hammering in her chest and her pulse pounding in her throat.

"Did I hurt you? Are you okay? Was that okay?" Riam asked, rolling onto his side to face her. He was nervous that he had rushed things, that somehow she would be broken all over again.

Sasha smiled, lifting her arm and almost slapping his cheek. "Sorry. My arms weigh a ton." She laughed. "That was perfect, and no, you didn't hurt me. That was amazing, Riam."

Riam sighed in relief. When he tried to move again, he felt the same as she had. "My legs feel like someone is sitting on them."

"I love you, Riam," Sasha whispered, lifting her head to kiss him.

"And I, you," Riam replied, turning his head to see Sid standing a few feet away.

"No, no, continue, I'm enjoying the free porn," Sid said with a smile.

Sasha lifted up onto her elbows and smiled, exposing her nude body. "You picked the wrong two people to try to embarrass. Seers are not ashamed of sexuality, nor are any of them monogamous."

"So, Riam, mind if I go a round or two with your Fyrvor?" Sid asked, trying to stir something inside Riam.

Riam smiled. "It's not up to me. If she's down with it, go right ahead. Hurt her and I'll kill you. Pleasure her and I'll owe you."

Sid stepped toward them, pulling his shirt up and over his head. "Last chance to back out, big guy."

"Toss me my clothes and I'll give you two some privacy," Riam said, leaning toward his pants.

Sid growled and pulled his shirt back on. "You two are no fun. Get your naked asses dressed, Cael has called a meeting. We have the location of Deagon's new warehouse."

Sasha gave Sid a wink. "I knew you wouldn't do it."

"And if I had?" Sid asked.

"I'm sure you'd have been a perfect gentleman, in your own twisted way."

Sid smiled, giving both Sasha and Riam a look at the man he really was. "I'd never dishonor your body, Sasha. I'm a whore, nothing more, and you deserve better."

Riam helped Sasha stand, but before dressing, she hugged Sid. "You and I know what kind of a man you are. A whore is not on that list. I'll keep your secret, though. You can be the leech you pretend to be and I won't tell anyone that you love each and every one in that house."

Sid pulled away, rolling his eyes. "Love? I'm only here for the free food, booze and fighting. I am man, hear me roar."

Riam and Sasha walked behind Sid, back to the compound.

The entire walk was filled with Sid listing off the names of everyone he'd slept with his first month out. The list was long, longer than Riam had expected. It didn't make Sid a whore. It made Riam realize how lonely Sid was. It also made him see just how much he'd given up, to stick with the Slayers, to stay with Des. Now that was love in its purest form.

Chapter Sixteen

"I can do this, Riam," Sasha said, yet felt like she was going to vomit on his shoes.

They all had been called back to the compound. As soon as they got in, they were suiting up for an attack on a warehouse owned by Deagon. They had confirmed intel that Deagon was setting up shop, housing tainted drugs, weapons and a suspicion that he had found a way to rebuild the Rancor Order and worse, Proletaryans. Recently Deagon had been seen with a few known black magick dealers, trying to track someone who could help him rebuild his shambling army. It was a risk The Netherworld wouldn't take.

"Why doesn't Warner just off him?" Zy had asked Cael.

"They want him alive, but they'll take him in a body bag as a last resort. They want the intel, and having a pulse makes it easier for Des to read them."

Every Slayer was out in full gear, ready to bring the warehouse to the ground. Sasha was among them. She had whispered to herself the entire time, pausing at the compound to contact Opal. She needed reassurance. Opal didn't have any answers, only Sasha had those answers. If it felt right, do it. If she had even the slightest hint that she was wrong, she shouldn't go and neither should anyone else.

Arriving at the warehouse, Riam had pulled her aside, saying he was concerned that this would be too much for her.

"Riam, I'm good to go. If I feel I can't do it, I will take post at the door. Cael and I have already discussed this. I'm solid and I'm ready," Sasha answered.

Riam tilted his head. "You look like you're gonna to upchuck. Are you sure?"

Sasha smiled. "Do you know how long it's been since I've played war games? I'm just a little nervous, okay? The thought that I'll get shot is what's making me wanna puke. When's the last time you were shot? For me, it was last year and it hurt like a bitch."

Riam kissed her forehead. "I love you."

"I love you too. Now go. You're embarrassing me in front of everyone else. Do you see anyone else's boyfriend giving them a pep talk?" Sasha asked, blushing.

"Boyfriend?" Riam whispered, grinning. "Are we going steady now?"

"Shut up and go away," Sasha said, shooing him.

Des leaned in from behind. "Actually, we all do. Cael gives me the same pep talk, even though I can protect myself better than he can. I mean, I have a freakin' Watchyr at my back and can die over and over again and make someone eat their own gun, but he still worries."

"I crawl on my hands and knees, begging Neri to stay home, every single time. I've even tried crying to keep her from coming," Zylan piped up. "But here she is, on top of the fucking building, ready to drop in from the top. We don't pair up with our partners for that reason. We won't focus. That's why you've been paired up with Bane. He'll work his ass off to keep you alive, and he won't get shot in the process."

Bane jogged up from the rear. "All set?"

Sasha gave him a nod. "I might puke."

Bane winked at her. "We all did the first time. Don't worry about it. Just try to aim it away from me and we're golden."

"Fuck, I hate this," Riam grumbled, jogging away, Bellum at his side.

The world seemed to speed up, everyone moving in at once. She followed Bane and ignored the rest. It was too much to focus on. They moved into the warehouse quietly but made one hell of a ruckus once they were inside. Her ears filled with screams and sounds of things breaking. Sasha dropped to the floor and covered her ears.

She opened her eyes when she was being pulled out of the way. Bellum had picked her up and moved her against the wall.

"Stay here," Bellum whispered. "It's okay, Sasha. Not being able to charge in to kill everything with a pulse is a good thing."

"I can do this," Sasha whispered, not believing her own words.

Bellum smiled. "I know you can, but you don't have to. Let me do this for you, please. Let me be the one to carry this burden. It would be an honor."

Sasha nodded. She wanted to be big and tough, kick ass and take names, but she couldn't push herself to move away from the wall.

Bellum lifted Sasha's gun and clicked off the safety. "If you don't know them, shoot them. Got it? I'll come back for you. Count to ten and I'll be back."

Sasha nodded again and watched Bellum move into the shadows. Each time Sasha counted to ten, Bellum would emerge from the darkness. Sasha would begin counting again and Bellum would leave. She returned, pulling a woman behind her.

"Sasha, I need you to get her out of here. Can you do that?" Bellum asked.

Sasha nodded and grabbed the woman from Bellum. Slowly, in the shadows of the warehouse, Sasha carried the woman over her shoulder, heading for the door. Seeing the exit, Sasha pushed forward, trying not to run. She didn't want to draw attention. Beside the door, two men whispered to each other. They were sneaking in behind the Slayers. She scanned the warehouse. She was the only one to notice them.

Fuck. She couldn't stand there forever. Her shoulder was tired from the weight of a full-grown adult. Hybrid or not, shit still got heavy, even for the best of them.

Sasha leaned into the wall, using it to help her balance the body. She had done this hundreds of times. She gave herself a pep talk. She knew she had to fire her weapon. She didn't want to but knew she had no other choice. Talking a calm breath, she raised her gun and fired two rounds. *Bang, bang.* She was in the zone. She kept moving toward the door, her ears wide open and eyes perfectly adjusted to the darkness. She turned once and fired again before making it outside. She carried the woman behind a set of pallets and took up post by the door. If they weren't friendly, she would be taking them down without pause.

Time had all but stopped for her outside, alone, in the dark. She wasn't afraid this time. She waited. She took down three more outside by the time Riam finally found her. He stepped out of the door and Sasha fired a round into the metal frame of the door.

"Oops," Sasha called out. "My bad."

Riam poked his head out the door, giving her a look and shaking his head. "Are you crazy?"

"Pretty much." Sasha laughed, feeling instant relief.

Bellum was behind, grinning. "You did it, Sasha. I knew you could. I never doubted you for a second."

"Yes, you did, your exact words were '*great, we're all going to die now*', or something like that," Sid said, walking behind Bellum.

"I did not, you lying sack of shit," Bellum said, pausing to elbow him in the ribs. "I said it was great that she was coming, less chance of all of us dying."

"I was paraphrasing," Sid countered, winking at Sasha.

Each one of them had this way of making her feel like she was one of them, even when they were in the middle of a shit storm.

Riam got to her front and pulled her into a tight hug. "We need to leave now."

"I disagree," Bellum spoke up from behind him. "Let her decide, Riam. Let her choose her own destiny. You do not have the right to take this from her."

133

Riam turned and glared at Bellum. "And you need to mind your fucking business."

Sasha pulled back, her eyes darted from Riam to Bellum. "What's going on?"

Bellum pushed past Riam. "We have Deagon. Des is going to interrogate him. Once that's over, we will end his life. I thought we should give you the option to be there. Maybe you, Des and Neri could rock-paper-scissors to see who gets to pull the trigger?"

Sasha staggered backward. Her heart jumped into her throat. She had dreamed of this very moment, had wanted nothing more than to take his life in a brutal attack. She had even come up with well-thought-out plans on how to slowly kill him in the most painful of ways that would last days.

She breathed in deeply then shook her head. "I do not wish to be the one to end his life nor do I want to watch it happen, but I do want to ask him one question before his life is ended."

Riam breathed a sigh of relief. "Thank God."

Sasha smiled. "I can't be there. I'm scared I'll enjoy it. I'm scared it'll remove all of my hard work and put me back at square one. I'm not willing to sacrifice another day for him. He gets nothing more from me."

The Slayers left the warehouse, taking the drugs, money and weapons with them. Deagon was tied up and gagged, riding in the back seat of Bane's truck, a Slayer on each side. In the front beside Bane, Neri and Des sat, both turned around looking at Deagon with ear-to-ear smiles. Sasha declined that ride and rode with Riam in his truck, with Amity and Sid.

Chapter Seventeen

Deagon hunched over on his knees. Des held on to his cheeks and look him dead in the eyes. Sid and Riam held on to her shoulders, helping her ride the wave of evil that was once Strain. Deagon tried squirming. He gave up once he grew tired and realized it was pointless.

Des let go of Deagon and backed up, still smiling. Riam had felt her emotions. She was disgusted and hated him, but she didn't want to be the one to pull the trigger. She didn't want to carry his death with her. It was bad enough she had suffered at his hands. She didn't want to suffer in her future because she had taken the life of an unarmed man. To Riam, he was armed, with hate and evil. But Des didn't see it that way.

Bellum moved into view of Deagon. "My brother, how far you've fallen."

Deagon smiled. "Sister, I could say the same. Slumming it, I see."

"Do you have any last words, before your life is extinguished and you are sent back to the darkness?" Bellum asked.

He looked around Bellum to Des and Cael. "I never risked sticking my cock in her mouth. Care to share? Is she any good?"

Des' grin widened. "Naturally, you've raved about how good I am in bed. I'm even better at foreplay."

Deagon's eyes turned to Neri. "Well hello, my little China doll."

"I'm not yours and I'm Korean, you dumb fuck." Neri laughed him off, and looked to Zylan. "How do so many people confuse the two?"

Zylan shrugged. "Lack of education or just plain ignorance."

Sasha came out from behind Riam's back, staring Deagon in the eyes. "Why did you take my family from me? I was told it was a mistake, but I'm no fool. Why?"

Deagon laughed. "Because I could."

"You lie, even now at the end?" Sasha asked.

Deagon shrugged. "I would sooner take that knowledge to my grave than allow you that peace of mind."

Des started laughing. "You take nothing to your grave, hotshot. Sasha, he ordered the death of you, not your family. His father had planned to mate with you, to create another Strain. He wanted you out of the picture. He didn't want the competition. Even then, the Genesys knew of you. The future was already written. Deagon tried to take you out but didn't have the power to alter destiny. So yes, it was an accident that your family perished, because *you* were his target."

Deagon glared at Des then back to Sasha, laughing. "It couldn't have worked out any better, actually."

Sasha nodded and stepped back. "I forgive you, Deagon."

"I don't need your fuckin' forgiveness, bitch." Deagon spat.

Sasha grabbed on to Riam's hand. "I'm not doing it for you. It is I who need to forgive. I cannot move on with that hate. It is my gift to you during your journey to your next life, all of that hate. Goodbye, Deagon."

Deagon moved to stand, to lunge at Sasha when Bellum's gun went off. Bellum shot her brother in the heart, two feet in front of Riam. Riam pulled Sasha into his chest, burying her face. He didn't want her to see it. She hadn't wanted to be present for his death, but here she was.

Sasha clung to Riam. "Take me away from here, Riam. I don't want to see this."

"I've got it from here," Bellum called out. "I'm sorry, Sasha. I couldn't let him touch you again. I'm so sorry."

Sasha nodded and let Riam pull her away from Deagon's dead body. Riam felt her flinch as Bellum pumped three more bullets into her brother.

"Get down." Bellum's scream echoed through the field.

Riam didn't ask questions. He hit the deck and took Sasha with him. He covered her body with his and waited.

"Daughter of mine, it has been many moons," the Genesys said.

His words felt like daggers on Riam's brain. His ears twitched, threatening to bleed. The urge to vomit from what felt like room spins, had pushed him to keep his head down.

"Father, have you come for Strain?" Bellum asked, unaffected by the voice of her father.

"I've come for Sasha. She is mine," the Genesys answered.

Riam watched as a thick dark fog rolled toward him and Sasha. The fog moved the way the smoke rolled from a fire, systematically crawling outward, seeking more oxygen. Riam held on to Sasha even tighter, knowing she would be bruised the following day, if they lived that long. He knew he wouldn't let her go. Even in death, his grip would remain. He prayed. He called out to the Orygin for aid.

As soon as the fog touched Riam and Sasha with a cold so frosty that it burned, they both flinched. Bellum let out a war cry. The sound echoed until it hit the fog. The darkness ate it up as if it had never happened. She fired her gun twice, sending the fog back from them. Riam twisted his head and watched Bellum charge into the fog, her gun going off again.

"You overstep every time, Bellum. For this, I take back my Strain," the Genesys said. A bony white hand emerged from the fog and grabbed Bellum by the throat.

Riam watched as a stream of darkness was sucked out of Bellum's mouth as she screamed. Her eyes bulged and her body contorted into angles no person should be in. The Genesys dropped Bellum to her feet, kicking her in the stomach and sending her across the grass as if it were ice. The fog rolled forward, twisting around everyone who took cover, coiling over Deagon and devouring him.

"You all will die for this," the Genesys said, his words cutting Riam's flesh.

Bellum lifted her bloodied arm and fired the last rounds in her gun. "Stone of the darkness. Heal that, motherfucker."

The fog rolled back into itself as a scream that Riam swore only dogs, and probably Bane, could hear echoed through the field. The tail end of it made them all scream in pain, a million tiny lashes landing on their brains.

Riam rolled off Sasha, her face stained with grass and blood. Sasha crawled forward, coughing up blood, to grab on to Bellum.

"Bellum, say something," Sasha yelled, pulling Bellum into her lap. "Please, say something."

The others rushed to Bellum, Neri pushing them to the side to get a look at her. Neri slapped Bellum across the face.

Bellum's eyes jerked open. "What the fuck is wrong with you? Any chance you get to hit someone, you take it?"

Neri laughed. "Wouldn't you?"

Bellum rolled off Sasha's lap, agreeing with Neri. "Holy shit. He's gonna be pissed off."

"Did you kill him?" Sasha asked.

Bellum shook her head. "I wish. No, but it'll take him a bit to heal the damage." Bellum looked around the field, frowning then closing her eyes with a groan.

"Yeah, about that... Your father did a dine and dash with Deagon," Sid said, stepping up without a single scratch on him.

"Fuck." Bellum groaned again. "He'll heal my brother and send him back. I was about to burn the body, so there would be nothing left, but then the father of all darkness popped in for a family reunion."

"What did he do to you?" Sasha asked.

"Daddy took little war's privileges away. She's been grounded," Sid answered, grinning.

Bellum nodded. "My father has the ability to remove his Strain from me and put it back in, if he so chooses. I thought my wards would protect me. But I also never thought I'd jump into him willingly to shoot him in the head, either."

Sasha touched Bellum on the shoulder and gave her a sympathetic smile. "Thank you, for your sacrifice."

"I'm not done yet," Bellum said, standing up. "This is only the beginning."

Riam helped Sasha to her feet and walked her back to the truck. There was no talk about the night, on the way back to the compound. Riam held her under his arm, breathing her in, thankful they'd made it out alive. They knew the fight had just got real. They had taken it to a whole new level. Tonight, they would love each other and be grateful, for tomorrow was a new day with new threats and a seriously pissed-off darkness.

Chapter Eighteen

Deagon's eyes opened and he screamed, clawing at his chest.

"Mr. Jackston. Sir, it's okay. You're okay," a woman yelled, trying to hold his arms down to keep him from tearing off his flesh.

Deagon pushed her away from him and sat up, looking around the room he was in. Van Gen Hospital. He wondered how he'd gotten there. The last thing he remembered was being shot by his sister. As the lights had gone out, he vaguely recalled hearing the gnawing pain of his father's voice.

"Deagon!" Julian ran into the room at full speed. "Thank God you're alive."

Deagon leaned back into his pillows, his heart still hammering.

"We got it on tape," Julian whispered, leaning in. "There was no sound, and we edited certain parts, of course, but we've released it. It shows poor you being attacked by agents."

Deagon sighed and reached for the yellow mug of water on the table beside his bed. His throat felt like sand had taken up housing and was quenching its thirst on his tongue.

"Let me help you," Julian said, poking a straw into the water and bringing it to Deagon's face. "What the fuck happened? I watched the tape. A dozen fully armed and well-trained people don't just break into a warehouse, Deagon. Who the hell are they?"

Deagon cleared his throat and went with a partial truth,

one that painted him in a better light. "They work for The Netherworld. They're called Slayers. Their leader is my brother, an irregular. I've tried to take them out on my own, before they could kill me. They've been hunting me for a year now—longer if you count all of the years they didn't know that it was me heading up the Rancor Order. The Order's only mission is to take down The Netherworld and irregulars."

Julian pulled a chair up beside the bed, his eyes as wide as saucers. "Perfect. This is too fucking perfect. We can use this, Deagon. The Netherworld tries to take you out just hours after you give a speech for The Purity of Humanity. I've called a press conference. We're moving you out of here to a safe and secure location."

Deagon nodded. "How the hell did I get here?"

Julian shrugged. "You were found in the bathroom of the emergency room, unconscious and looking like you'd been beaten half to death."

Deagon pulled the IV from his arm and swung his legs out of bed. With the help of Julian, Deagon found himself standing in the bathroom, looking in the mirror. Each place his sister had shot him was a basketball-size, blackened bruise. No bullet wounds, though. He had three gigantic bruises on his body, and one on the side of his head. She'd meant business, three to the chest and one to the head. If she was out of exile, he wasn't safe anywhere.

His father was the only one who'd had the power to save him, to return his life. He wondered why he would help him, after royally screwing him to begin with. As thankful as he was to be alive, it scared him more to think he owed the Genesys a debt for saving his life. Daddy dearest clearly wanted something from him. Knowing the Genesys, that would be the only reason he had lifted a finger to help. The very thought made Deagon grab the toilet and evacuate the tiny bit of water in his stomach.

"I don't care who you are, Mr. Marshal. You'll be stepping aside before your pretty little chicklet teeth are scattered across this floor."

Deagon lifted his head with a grin. Prudence was here.

"Ma'am, if you could please just step outside. I will ask Mr. Jackston if he is receiving guests at this time," Julian said, in his best calming-the-crazy-white-girl voice.

Prudence laughed. "I will count to three. On three, you'll be thankful we're inside of a hospital."

"Let her in, Julian," Deagon called from the bathroom.

Part of him wanted to see Prudence in action. Could she really follow through or was she all talk? She gave him a look filled with worry, but under that, it was all disappointment. Prudence turned on the water, running a cloth under the stream. It had felt like heaven the moment she touched the back of his neck with it.

Prudence leaned into his ear, gripping the back of his neck through the cloth. "Deagon, you know how much I appreciate you for giving me and my children a chance, right? I bust my ass every day for you, putting in about eighty hours a week. I'm on call for you around the clock and I have done shit I didn't think I could — or would — even dare to do. I have cleaned up your messes, including the ones you should damn well rot in jail for. And for what? You never fucking learn. You want to run drugs? Fine, awesome, perfect. But you're too stupid to do it in a way that doesn't land you in the hospital. You want to create a little band of thugs? Great. But you're too fucking arrogant to do it the right way. You want power? Each time you get some, you fucking choke on it."

"It's great to see you too, Pru." Deagon spoke, his voice echoing inside of the toilet.

"You run your streets like a playground, picking on the weak and taking their lunch money. You will never have the power until you're willing to do it for reasons other than revenge. Stop running around with a hard-on for Des and a death wish for Cael. That will come when your power base is actually powerful. You're being stupid and I won't fuckin' die for a fool."

Prudence stopped pushing his head into the toilet, pulling his face up to look her in the eyes. She dabbed the cloth over his forehead, glaring.

"Do I make myself clear, Deagon?" she asked. "Answer me or I start flushing the toilet, with your head in it, buried ears deep. You're not the only one with something to lose here. My entire life, the future for my children, all rests on your ability to man the fuck up. First it's your daddy issues, then it's your brother issues, then it's Desdemona, then it's your Order, then it's enough cocaine to bake a cake, then it's this and that and the list goes on and fucking on. You think you're the only one in this world who has been screwed over? Every time you sink your cock into some whore, have you ever stopped to wonder how they got there? Good times and golden roads didn't lead them to their knees in front of the likes of you. Trust me on that. No sane person wants to be closed into a room with you, Deagon. We all know what you're about and only the most desperate are willing. That should tell you a little something about yourself as well."

Deagon pulled his head back and nodded. "Have I ever told you how much I fucking hate you?"

Prudence grinned. "Every time I spit the truth in your face."

"I'm fucked, Pru," Deagon whispered, looking at the floor. He could feel the weight of his world kicking him in the balls, one nut at a time.

Prudence stood and put her purse on the counter. "Six ways from Sunday, Deagon. And stop calling me Pru. You know I hate it."

Deagon watched her put on eyeliner and mascara then drip water over her eyes. "What are you doing?"

"I'm distraught. You're my boss and I've been waiting for the phone call to tell me that they found you, dead. The media is on their way. You need supporters, Deagon, and you'll never find them with your stupidity leading the way. Go get dressed. I dropped a duffle bag by the bed."

Deagon lifted himself off the floor and paused before

leaving the bathroom. "Thank you, Pru… Prudence."

She turned her head and rolled her eyes. "Don't think I'm doing this for you, hot stuff. I don't want to die because of you, and I can't afford to leave my job."

Deagon smiled, knowing she was full of shit. He left her to create the perfect wounded bird. A woman in pain would grip the hearts of everyone. He got dressed, surprised at himself for thanking her. He had to be honest. He appreciated Prudence. She had a set of balls that made even the biggest man at the club cower. The security, which was trained to kill, didn't go up against her. It wasn't her size or her skill that made them tremble. It was the look in her eyes. She was a fighter, and she was willing to fight to the death for every inch. Anyone willing to die was a scary motherfucker.

Julian pushed in a wheelchair and Deagon climbed aboard. "Ready?"

Deagon nodded.

"I'm ready," Prudence said, stepping out of the bathroom.

Her makeup had been cleaned up a bit, but it had looked like she had spent the last day bawling her eyes out. Her hair was pulled up into a messy bun and her clothes looked wrinkled like she'd slept in them. As if on cue, Prudence gripped Deagon's hand and let the waterworks begin. The three of them pushed out of the room.

Outside the front doors of Van Gen Hospital, a few dozen reporters waited for Deagon. The questions bombarded him from all sides. They wanted to know what had happened, but no one wanted to hear any form of truth. They wanted a story that made headlines and sold papers, nothing more. Julian fielded questions about Deagon's apparent drug trafficking, arms dealing and sex trade. The Netherworld had released a statement, following the release of the surveillance tape that showed his warehouse under attack. The Netherworld had sent in agents to disband a newly formed gang, nothing more. That was their stand on the attack.

The media was basically given the truth on a silver platter, yet wanted more. His tragic side, as if he would cough up anything that resembled the truth. But they kept pushing, asking for comments.

"Stop it. Just stop it," Prudence cried. She had realized things were going downhill and fast. As she spoke, the pitch of her voice rose and sounded more like angry screaming in the end. "You paint him as a monster. He was the only person to help me. When I was on my knees, trying to earn enough money to feed my children, he rescued me. He saved me and my children. He paid off my bills and mortgage. He went hungry so my kids and I could eat. He stopped me from having to do some of the most shameful acts, just to give my children running water. How dare you say those things about him? How dare you!"

Deagon stood and glared at the reporters, pulling Prudence into his arms. "You have nothing to be ashamed of, Pru. You did everything you could to save yourself and your family. Never be ashamed of that and never allow others to dictate who you are. You are strong. You are a survivor, and I could only hope to become someone like you."

Prudence buried her face into Deagon's chest, her shoulders shaking with her sobs. Deagon wondered for a moment if her tears were real, if she honestly was ashamed. But he knew better than that. She was damn strong and more of a survivor than Deagon would ever be.

Deagon turned to the cameras and spoke softly. "Prudence finds the best in people, even when there is nothing left to see. Yet, she cannot see the best of herself. Was I a drug lord? No, not even close. But I did run drugs, like every other lost soul down Blood Alley, trying to make enough money to eat. Did I work in the sex trade? Yes, and I still do. I still try to make sure sex trade workers are safe and not being abused. You call that being a pimp? Well then, I wish the streets were filled with more of those kinds of pimps and not just the ones who sell the souls of the desperate. You say

I am forming a gang on the backs of the underprivileged? Go to the warehouse. I invite you to come. Well, what's left of it. It's a piss-poor home I have tried to give them. It's a roof over their heads and food in their bellies. It isn't to form a gang. It is to give them somewhere to feel safe. Their payment to me for my kindness is community service. Ask any one of them. To get in the door they must bring with them two bags of trash off our streets. You've seen pictures of the warehouse. It's barely one step up from a crack shack, but it's still better than what they had. And I'm proud to say that I helped them. I'm proud of who they are trying to become. Most of them have returned to school and have gotten jobs, because they no longer have to worry about where their next meal is coming from."

Deagon willed his eyes to form tears. "I was attacked and those I promised to keep safe were shot and killed. And why? Because The Netherworld and their little band of killers think I'm a threat. They charged in and shot children. They were just kids, God damn it. I did everything I could to protect them and it wasn't enough. Do I feel responsible for their deaths? Yes, completely. I gave them my word and I failed them. I wish I would have died with them. At least I would have kept my word. I wouldn't have had to wake up to the knowledge that they died, trying to protect me."

Deagon pushed his head into Prudence's hair, racked with a false sense of grief. He almost laughed out loud, knowing that moment had been one of his all-time best acts.

"They were only children," Deagon sobbed. "I failed them. I couldn't save them."

Julian stepped forward and touched Deagon's shoulder. "As you see, folks, he is just a man trying to make his neighborhood safer for those who call it home. He was attacked following our gala, for speaking out against The Netherworld. As you saw from the footage released, Mr. Jackston was pulled out of the warehouse, kicking and screaming. He tried to go back in for them, but the agents bound and gagged him and threw him into a truck. If it wasn't for the kindness of a complete stranger bringing him to the hospital, he'd be dead. Almost twenty souls — those Mr. Jackston had sworn to protect — were slaughtered in their sleep, by those claiming to be called Slayers. They claimed to work for The Netherworld. Is this what we pay our taxes for? The Netherworld killing our children as they sleep in their beds at night? Beds Mr. Jackston paid for with his own money. He has gone hungry for our children, and our own government sends in assassins to take them out. I, for one, am disgusted."

Prudence helped Deagon sit back in his wheelchair. "It'll be okay, Deagon. We'll find a way to pay for their funerals. I have some jewelry I can sell, and that television you purchased for my kids? We don't need it. My car is an old one, but it still runs. I'll list it tonight."

Deagon looked up at Prudence with a smile. "No. I will not take from you or your children. We'll find a different way to honor them."

Julian pushed Deagon away from the media who were still screaming questions, toward the black SUV double-parked in the lot. Prudence helped Deagon climb into the back seat, slowly and painfully. Closing the door, the act was over.

"Your car is brand-fucking-new, off the lot. I should know. I paid for it," Deagon said. "I didn't buy your kids a television, I checked my VISA statement. You purchased a fucking in-house theater system."

Prudence smiled. "Did you see their faces? Not a dry eye in sight."

Julian turned from the front seat as they pulled away. "I like you, Prudence. You're good for his image. Keep it up."

Prudence leaned forward. "If there's one thing I've learned from Deagon, it's that nothing is free. I'm not a volunteer. If you want my time, you pay for it. I do my volunteering elsewhere."

Julian nodded and Prudence leaned back into her seat with a yawn. No words were exchanged between the two for the rest of the drive. Deagon was surprised by her little act, but at the same time, he didn't doubt her abilities to survive one bit. They dropped her off at the club, then Julian took Deagon to a five-star hotel downtown. The Purity of Humanity had rented him a suite for the month. He didn't bother asking who was bankrolling his new digs. He didn't care.

"The donations are pouring in," Julian said, opening the door for Deagon. "You have fresh clothes in the bedroom closet. Order what you want. We have you covered. You'll have a security detail in the hall for whenever you need to leave."

Deagon gave him a nod then closed the door. He needed a shower, a whore and a drink. His shower, although it was like a tropical waterfall, gave him no pleasure. The drink did nothing either, nor did the sixth one. With a hooker face down, ass up, his hand pushing her face into the pillow, it barely moved him. It was one of the first times he truly had to work for his orgasm. It was the first time he had to let her lift her head from the pillow, the first time he didn't call her a dirty whore and the first time he didn't crunch up the bills to toss them on the floor.

He sent her on her way, turned on all of the lights then sat with a bottle of rye, alone. Prudence was right. He was blindly stumbling through life, allowing his hate to guide him. He would never become anything more than he was in that moment, unless he screwed his head on straight and got his shit together. It was easier said than done. Years of learned behavior had to be erased. He had to start over, new, sober and level-headed.

Sure, he would always be a bastard and would never outgrow his hatefulness. Those characteristics were a part of his DNA. But he had to be more methodical than this. He had to plan. He put his head in his hands and cursed. He had to do what his father had been trying to teach him. His ears twitched with the faintest of laughter in the air. He knew his father was laughing at him. He took another pull from his bottle and stuck his middle finger in the air.

"Fuck you," Deagon cursed.

He screwed the cap on the bottle, stood up and headed to his club. He had work to do, planning to take care of and more fighters to acquire. He finally saw the bigger picture and he was chasing it. It had only taken his father damn near killing him, followed by the Slayers attacking and his sister pumping bullets into his body. Like most things in life, lessons were always learned the hardest way possible. At least in his case, that was his experience.

The Slayers would go down. But bigger than that, The Netherworld needed to crumble. He wouldn't do it in his usual fashion. No. He would do it the legal way. He would take the route that was public and allow doubt to spread through those who voted. He would bring The Purity of Humanity to the top and have them do his dirty work. He'd play the biggest victim while being the foremost predator.

He walked through Blood Alley, as he had hundreds of times before, only this time, he had four men trailing him for protection. He breathed in the sickness in the air and his stomach turned. Hookers shambled from cock to cock with their greedy mouths wide open, while dirty needles were passed from vein to vein. His little chunk of the city was a cesspool, all but forgotten and hated by those who remembered. Every alleyway had housed its fair share of death, most of which could still be tasted in the air. The sidewalks were littered. What was left of the humanity in those parts had lined the concrete with trash.

It was perfect. It was home. The show must go on. First things first, he would recreate the Proletaryans. He needed his army back, and he knew of a witch who could help him. He just needed a way to force her hand. Everyone had a weakness, which was his specialty — forcing someone to see things his way.

Chapter Nineteen

Riam gripped Sasha's hand as they walked through the field behind the compound. The night had been perfectly breathtaking in all of its sadness and laughter. The Slayers had helped Sasha with her final goodbyes, gathering for a funeral for people they had never met. But by knowing Sasha and caring for her, they had circled around her for support. It wasn't anything fancy. It was simply a goodbye, but that was all that was needed.

Each person had spoken about someone they had lost, told their most precious memory and said their own goodbyes. The night had somehow felt lighter, like they had been carrying around the weight of their backbreaking sorrow until the moment they said their farewell out loud.

Sasha had said goodbye to her family and welcomed her new one. She spoke about who she had become because of the anger she'd carried and let go of the hateful warmth it had brought her. Riam watched as her shoulders became straighter, lighter, as the pain departed.

Des had spoken about Zoe, her one true friend. She smiled now, when she spoke of Zoe and could even laugh at the train wreck of a person Zoe—who had trampled through life without a care—was. Des had loved that most about her friend, how free she was with life. The smile she held became more solid, truer, as the sadness crept away.

Cael had said goodbye to his brother. The Deagon he had known and loved was long gone, lost to the darkness. Riam watched Cael talk about Deagon, his eyes still lighting up with love. Bellum had been on board with Cael, saying goodbye to her brother and was thankful for being a part of this new family, invited in as a Slayer. She said that for once, she had felt like she belonged to something important, with people who were important.

Zylan and Neri both said goodbye to lost family and embraced their new one. Both were still madly in love and fiercely protective of that love and the family they had left. Amity had joined them both, grieving the past lives lost at Sola-Nosfer, and she was thankful for the new laws that protected the Vestal Virgyns. Zylan's mother ruled her society with an iron fist, a kind one, but unforgiving when it came to abuses on her people.

Bane couldn't choose just one, so he had said goodbye to fallen pack members. He mourned those who had died helping the Slayers and those who had died from the hate of others. He ended his words with a howl that had made the others smile and tear up.

Riam had said goodbye to the man he used to be, the man that had held the pain from every war and every death. He had spoken of that man's courage and honor. He had said goodbye to the sadness his inner warrior carried and welcomed the beginning of a new life, with his Fyrvor. He had forgiven himself, for breaking his word to his sister, as he'd said goodbye to her. He would leave it all behind in the field and learn to love himself as much as he loved Sasha.

But it was Sid who had blown everyone away with his words. When it came time for Sid to speak, Riam had braced himself for another tall tale of hookers and coke, ten-dollar blowjobs and waking up in ditches. Instead, he was moved at just how much love Sid had, for everyone. The burden he carried, and the fight he fought with every step he took.

"I have far too many people to list. There are too many people who I have held during their last moments and those who I had tried to save, but failed. I have been there during all of your moments. Each time you had lost a loved one, I was there and I mourned that death with you. I have done everything I could, with everything in my power, to keep this pain from each of you. I have made bargains and have crawled through glass to keep pain from your door." Sid looked up to the sky and sighed. "If I had to choose what I'm saying goodbye to, I'd choose love. I once knew a girl. Man, she was a knockout. But it wasn't her looks that attracted me to her. It was her soul and the way it touched mine, the softest of caresses that made my world stand still and make perfect sense. It was how she forgave me when even I couldn't forgive myself. It was how she loved me when no one else would."

"What?" Des whispered. "What happened?"

Sid dropped his gaze from the sky and smiled. "In a way, I sacrificed that love to keep her alive. For me, getting too close can be the end to those I care for. I gave the only sacrifice worth giving. I gave my heart to keep hers beating. I will mourn for all of my days. It is a pain that time won't heal. It kills me every day, but I'd don't regret it."

Des reached for Sid, hugging him. "I never knew. I'm so sorry, Sid."

Sid lifted Des' chin and smiled. "I'm not sorry. The part that makes this the hardest is that I'd do it again. Even now, knowing the pain my soul would feel, I would do it again without pause. Knowing she is alive and happy, I'd do it a million times over."

"I love you," Des said and kissed Sid's cheek. "I love you more than life."

Riam's eyes almost bulged out of his head when he watched Sid kiss Des on the lips.

"I love you too," Sid said.

Riam tensed when Cael moved in. He thought for sure Cael would beat the fallen Watchyr with a rock, for kissing his Fyrvor on the lips. Instead, Cael hugged Sid and kissed him square on the lips. Everyone went silent and stared. The three of them stood in an embrace, whispering their love for one another.

"Well, this is a little awkward. Do we beat Sid up for touching Des or do we wait for the three-way to begin?"

Bane asked Riam, nudging him with his elbow, sporting an ear-to-ear grin.

Sid laughed and pulled back from Des. "You wish, pup."

Bane lifted his chin to the sky and howled.

Des pulled away, holding hands with Sid and Cael. "You're hanging out with Sid far too much if you think you're getting to watch us."

No one asked them if they actually did have sex. No one cared. If they did, great. If they didn't, that worked too. If Cael and Sid wanted to toss off their clothes and bend over a log, no one would care. There wasn't a soul in this field who would judge them or love them any less. Cael would always be their Aegys, Sid would always be a leech, and Des would always scare the fucking hell out of everyone here.

They had ended the funeral with a celebration. This wasn't the end. This was a new beginning for them all. They shed the sorrow and left it in the field behind them.

"Thank you, Riam," Sasha whispered and leaned her head on his shoulder. "I needed this."

Riam smiled and pulled her under his arm He held her against him and walked back to the compound, back to their home. "I think we all needed this."

Bane charged past them with a growl. "I have a date."

"With who?" Riam asked. "And where? You know the drill."

Bane turned, jogging backward, facing Riam. "I think I'm the only one here that follows the rules."

"No, you don't." Sid laughed, jogging up to Bane's side and pushing him over.

Bane rolled onto the ground and was back on his feet. Then he gave Sid the bird. "Most of them, but that should say a lot about the rest of you."

"Where are you going and who are you taking?" Riam called out, feeling protective of Bane.

"Midnight picnic, we'll be in wolf territory. She doesn't know about me. We should be safe there. I've already cleared it with my Alpha," Bane said.

Riam nodded. Bane wasn't a fool. He was foolish at times, but he wasn't the type to risk an innocent. Bringing the date into wolf territory would keep her safe, as well as Bane.

Bane stopped jogging in circles around them. "Riam, should I cancel? I mean, she doesn't smell like a threat, but I've never gone out with a human before. Do you think I'm leading danger to my people?"

"I've never dated a human before, either. Trust your gut, wolf. Call if you need help and we'll come," Riam said. It was all he could say. If things didn't feel right, they probably weren't right.

Bane gave a nod, jumped in the air and clicked his feet together. "See you in the morning."

Riam and Sasha watched Bane and Sid run the rest of the way to the compound. Sid taunted Bane and Bane tossed back a few of his own insults. They were regular comedic shit shows. Just as Sid was about to win, Bane lunged through the air and tackled Sid to the ground, gaining his lead.

"They're gonna to be the death of me," Cael piped up, walking with Des.

Riam turned with a grin. "You're the one fucking him, not me."

Cael nodded. "True." Then he smiled.

"Seriously? You're sleeping with Sid?" Riam asked, as his jaw dropped open.

"Would it matter?" Des asked.

"No, I guess it wouldn't," Riam answered, smiling.

Riam picked Sasha up to walk the rest of the way to the compound. The moment she was in his arms, the noise of the world went away. He couldn't keep his eyes off her or stop touching her. He had this fear that if he blinked for too long or let go of her hand, he'd wake up and it would all be a dream.

Back in the compound, Cael talked shop about the media coverage, with Deagon center stage. The Netherworld was going postal. The Slayers were ghosts, never to be brought to light, yet here they were, named on live television. Warner, their main contact, would be in touch. His ass was blistered from the hot water the Slayers had dropped him in with their raid on Deagon's warehouse.

The most recent footage showed Deagon holding a funeral for the fallen boys. He never once mentioned that each one had tried to take out the Slayers, or the fact that they had found ten kilos of uncut smack and enough weapons for a small army.

Each day following, for weeks, it would show Deagon and his boys cleaning up Blood Alley, painting over graffiti and feeding the homeless. Deagon's warehouse received a state-of-the-art facelift, along with a training center and top-notch security, courtesy of Julian and his raving lunatics. Deagon was actively holding conferences about the irregular gene, sponsored by The Purity of Humanity.

Essentially, Deagon just became one of the hardest bastards to kill. But like everything else in life, if there was a will, there was a way. They'd take him out or die trying.

Curled up behind Sasha, Riam kissed her shoulders, holding her head to the side by her hair. He pushed himself inside her. Her body pulled at him with its wetness. He locked his arm under hers, twisting at her hard nipples. She loved riding the line between pleasure and pain. Just a touch harder and she would come undone.

"I love you," he whispered into her ear.

"I love you too, lover of mine. Now fuck me," she commanded, pushing her hips into his.

"You asked for it," he said, biting her shoulder.

He pushed her hips forward, rolling her onto her stomach, and he climbed behind her. He yanked her hips into the air and slammed into her. He knew he would bottom out, her body was only so big and he was on the larger side, eleven inches with a girth she could barely swallow.

He twisted one fist in her hair, pulling her head back. He dug his nails into her hip and he fucked her. Their bodies slapped together, adding to her screams. She was a loud one when he fucked her. The first time had brought the Slayers into their bedroom. Neither she nor Riam had stopped the show.

"Close," Sasha screamed, her voice nothing more than a deep-bellied growl.

Riam let go of her hair and licked his thumb. He slid it around her waist to rub at her clit. She came undone, bucking against his cock. She pressed her face into the bed and screamed as her orgasm took hold. Riam could feel her pulse around his cock, begging for more. He worked himself over her sweet spot, feeling his balls tighten.

"Fuck," he screamed, filling her with his seed.

He felt his cock hit her cervix, back and forth. He swore he saw sound, his vision popping into bursts of stars. His legs turned to jelly and he fell to his side, as he tried to breathe.

Riam had learned that this would not be the end for Sasha, she was always greedy for more. She pulled him into her mouth until his heart threatened to explode, then she climbed onto his hips. Now, he would love her. Only now, after they had gotten their fill of dirty talk, rough sex and the pain she needed, they would make love.

He loved to watch her above him. The candlelight dancing across her skin, touching places his lips loved to venture. The way she would look at him would push the world away, leaving them alone together.

"I love you," she whispered, leaning down to his mouth.

He held her close to his heart, moving with her. Her orgasm didn't pound down on her as the one before. It came gently, caressing her every inch. It flowed from her body into his, pulling him with her. His body felt like it was floating, coated in pleasure. When they both came down together, he pulled her into his chest, their hearts beating in unison.

For the first time, in his entire life, curled around her, he loved someone with every fiber of his being. She was his safety, and he was hers. Never again would either of them face the harshness and cruelties that the world dished out. Finally, he had something worth living for and not just dying for.

"Now, go make me a sandwich, bitch." Sasha laughed, pushing him out of bed with her ice-cold feet.

Riam turned and playfully lifted his middle finger in the air. He knew Sasha would charge at him. And with screams, he ran from her. He wanted her to catch him. He needed to be caught. Feeling her grabbing him had grounded his soul. It reminded him that he had someone at his back, always. That feeling was enough to give him peace.

There was no better feeling in the world than to be needed, wanted and most of all, loved — loved when he was in his darkest hour, raging like a hurricane, and loved during the stillness of the day, when he shone as bright as the sun. The kind of true love that holds your hand and lifts you up, never remembering a past and only building on a future. That was what he found inside Sasha, and he'd protect that until the day he was burned and scattered.

Chapter Twenty

After three solid months working with Opal, Sasha had freed herself from the wounds of her past. With the night's meditation at an end, she stood up and wobbled on her feet. The room tilted and her stomach evacuated on the floor. With a death grip on the wall, Sasha froze in panic.

"Sasha, are you unwell?" Opal asked, already standing, touching Sasha's shoulder.

Sasha pulled away and shook her head. "No, this can't be. No, no, no."

Sasha darted from her bedroom and ran down the hall toward Des' bedroom. She didn't bother knocking. She knew Cael was on hunting duties, which left Des alone and likely reading a book or watching a movie.

Des jumped up and tossed her book onto the bed. "What's happened? Is it Cael? Tell me he's okay. Sweet Orygin, tell me my Cael is alive."

Sasha grabbed Des' hand and placed it on her stomach. "Tell me it's not darkness, Des. Please, tell me it's not a Strain."

Des frowned for a moment. She flinched as her ability of sight took her over. Des pulled her hand back. "What the hell, Sasha? You just scared the shit out of me. I don't see anything, aside from visions of your life prior to becoming a Slayer. I don't really see much from any of you. My abilities rarely work with those who are on the same path as me. I'm not like Sid or Riam."

"Am I pregnant?" Sasha whispered.

Des' eyes widened. She shrugged. "My sight doesn't work like that, Sasha. I can't pick and choose what to see like that on a whim. I'm not that powerful without Sid or Riam to help me. We need to go to Neri. She'll be able to see. Or to Riam or Opal."

Sasha shook her head. "No, not Riam. What if the child is not Riam's?"

"What makes you think you're pregnant?" Des asked.

"She became dizzy and ill to her stomach," Opal called out from the bedroom door.

"Get in here before everyone hears you," Sasha groaned and motioned for Opal to step into the bedroom.

Neri poked her head in the door. "Sasha, are you pregnant?"

"Fuck, this place is too fucking small," Sasha muttered. "I don't know."

Opal stepped forward with her hand stretched out toward Sasha's stomach. "I could check for you, should you wish it?"

Sasha nodded and lifted her arms. "Neri, I may need to terminate this pregnancy. Are you able to do that? I can't go ahead if there's a chance it's a Strain."

Neri stepped into the room and closed the door. "Your body, your choice, Sasha. I'm able to help you, but not with the equipment I have. We'll need a few extra items."

Opal's hand touched Sasha's stomach and a coolness rippled over Sasha's skin, making her shiver.

Opal pulled back with a nod. "Yes, you are pregnant."

"How far along? I need to know exactly," Sasha asked. Her face felt blistering hot, fresh tears poured down her cheeks.

"Of that, I can't be completely sure. You are in your first trimester. That is all I can tell," Opal answered.

"Let's get an ultrasound done. We'll know more then," Neri said, as she stepped toward the door.

"If you wish to terminate the pregnancy, I will assist. We have herbs for it," Opal said, and gave Sasha's arm a gentle squeeze.

Sasha followed Neri to her clinic, with a death grip on

Des' hand. Opal fhaded from the compound and would return with an herbal tea to aid Sasha. There was a time she thought she'd never have children again. She hadn't wanted to risk something precious in her life. Knowing a life was growing inside her made her soul smile just a little. But knowing it could potentially be a Strain made her heart heavy. Could she really end the life inside her? As much as she wanted to say she could, she knew she probably wouldn't when the time came.

Sasha climbed onto the small table and lifted her shirt. Neri sat on a stool to her right with Des' hand still locked firmly in place.

"Whatever happens, Sasha, you're not alone," Des said. A kind smile formed on her face as she spoke.

Sasha nodded and closed her eyes. She could feel the tears roll from the corners of each eye and pool in her ears. Opal returned with a small white-cloth bag, mentioning they were the herbs, should they be needed. She took position at the head of the bed then ran her hands through Sasha's hair, trying to keep her calm.

"This is going to be a little cold," Neri said and squeezed out a small package of lubrication onto Sasha's lower abdomen.

Sasha could feel the pressure of the ultrasound wand, pressing into her muscles.

"All right, let's see what we can see," Neri said.

Sasha listened to Neri mumble to herself, as she pushed the wand into her stomach a little deeper, trying to get a better view.

"Sasha, you appear to be about nine or ten weeks pregnant." Neri's words echoed in Sasha's ears.

"Are you sure? Like one hundred fucking percent positive?" Sasha asked.

"Not one hundred. But I'd say I'm one hundred percent sure you did not conceive during your time with the Genesys. You're not nearly far enough along for that."

Sasha nodded, her body relaxed into the table. She let out

a shaking breath and felt her shoulders let go of the tiny knots beginning to form. "Thank you, Orygin."

Des leaned forward, hugging Sasha. "Thank God."

Sasha sat up, nearly missing Des' head with her own. "Shit. Riam."

Sid, of perfect timing, stepped into the room. "Riam is on a warpath, Sasha. He keeled over in the field. He's on his way. He knows something is wrong."

Sasha jumped off the table, her stomach flopped again. She eyed up the wastebasket beside the bed then hunkered down for another round of stomach evacuation. She could feel Riam coming like a freight train.

"Do you want him in or out, Sasha?" Neri asked. "My clinic, my rules."

Sasha lifted her face, her cheeks wet with tears. "I don't know. I think maybe out. I mean, when he finds out, he's going to leave me. He doesn't want children. He doesn't want to bring another pure Seer into the world."

"Sid, man the door. No one gets in here. I don't care who it is," Neri ordered. Sasha watched her pull out her phone. "Zy, we need you back here. Riam is about to go postal and we need as many men as we can muster."

Sasha could hear Riam arguing with Sid. Bellum chimed in and guarded the door, which kept Riam from pushing his way through. She knew it would end up taking all of the Slayers to keep Riam from kicking his way into the room.

Opal rubbed her hand on Sasha's shoulders. "Give Riam a chance, Sasha. He loves you fiercely, and I think he would handle this as a perfect gentleman."

Sasha groaned into the wastebasket. She knew Opal was probably right.

"You won't be able to hide in here forever, Sasha." Des spoke as she moved toward the door. "What should I tell him? I have to give him something or he's going to kill to get in here. I know if it were me and Cael, he'd have used Sid's head as a battering ram by now."

Sasha stood and leaned forward on the bed, breathing

deeply. "Okay, I'm ready. Let's just get this over with."

Des cracked the door. "Sasha will see you now, but please know, if you get out of control in there, I'll make you think you're a little girl."

Sasha watched Riam storm into the clinic, his face twisted in anger until his eyes locked with hers. His anger melted and was replaced with concern.

"Fyrvor, what's happened?" Riam asked, and moved quickly through the room to grab on to her. Riam pulled her into his arms and locked them tightly around her. "Please, Sasha, what's happened? Whatever it is, it's okay. I'm here now."

Sasha pulled her face back, tears streamed down her checks. "I'm pregnant. I'm so sorry, Riam. I didn't mean for it to happen. I'm so sorry."

Riam frowned and looked to Neri. "How far along? I mean, it doesn't matter, but, how far?"

"I'm so sorry. I'll pack my things. You don't have to do this. I should have been more careful. I know you didn't want this," Sasha cried into his shoulder and tried to pull away.

Zylan had picked the perfect time to fhade into the room. He pulled Neri behind him and eyed up Riam for the possibility of trouble.

Neri poked her head around Zyland. "She's nine or ten weeks along."

Riam dropped to his knees, pressed his head into Sasha's stomach and clung to her hips. His shoulder's shook and it took him three tries before his words made any sense.

"Don't leave. Please, don't go. I am honored," Riam cried into Sasha's stomach. He glanced up, his tears glittering in the light. "I'm going to be a father."

Sasha dropped to her knees in front of him. "You're not going to leave me?"

"Dear Orygin, why would I leave you?"

"You said you never wanted children, that you never wanted this life for them. I thought you'd be angry with me."

Riam cupped her cheeks and kissed her. "I love you, Sasha. I couldn't be more proud or thankful. Marry me. Please, do me this honor."

"Yes, a million times, yes," Sasha cried. She clung to Riam's shoulders as he lifted her into his arms.

Riam moved through the room, his eyes locked on hers. He stopped at the door to see Cael grinning.

"I'm going to be a father," Riam said, his voice proud and strong. "I'm going to be a husband."

Cael clapped Riam on the back, his eyes filled with tears. "Congrats, my man."

Sasha held on to her mate as they walked back to their bedroom. The panic had melted the moment he had dropped to his knees in joy. Her heart was whole again. Her life was whole again.

She'd be a mother, once more. She'd been given the chance to be a wife to this man of hers. This was true fate. This was the path she was meant to be on. She'd never forget her old life and she would miss her family terribly, but it would help her appreciate every moment to come. And she'd certainly not take a single breath for granted. She spent the night with her soon-to-be husband, loving and looking forward to a new life.

Fate had taken from her, but fate had also given back. She had come full circle, climbing out of hell and into the arms of forever. She no longer wished for the wickedness that was all-consuming.

Riam held her hand and pushed a small golden band onto her finger. One ruby sat in the middle. It was his mother's and her mother's before her. Sasha would treasure it and pass it down to her daughter, if fate so decided.

Glossary of Terms

Aegys (n.): A protector, sponsorship or guardian. The literal translation is 'one who watches over another', used between parents, lovers and close friends. It is pronounced 'e-jis'.

The Calyph (pr. n.): The leader of the Rancor Order, a powerful figurehead that targets the irregular, metaphysical or inhuman. Their main goal is the extinction of The Netherworld Government.

Day Walkyr (n.): A human with Vampyre DNA, prior to their first death.

Elysium (n.): The Overworld inhabited by departed souls, also known as "heaven" in human cultures.

Fhade (v): To disappear, to become free of physical substance, cease to have material character or qualities. To materialize and dematerialize.

Fyrvor (n.): A term of endearment for a person you feel intense heat or love toward. It is a bond between two lovers. A bond felt by both, it is a continuous connection. Once broken, the wounds are for all time.

The Genesys (n.): The origin and creator of the Rancor Order, neither dead nor alive. Their children are known as a Strain, called solely 'Strain'. The Genesys is the first Prophetyc, the reason the Orygin has prohibited the mating between angels and demons. The Genesys chose the path of evil, activating the irregular gene within mankind.

Hades (n.): The Underworld inhabited by departed souls, also known as 'hell' in human cultures.

Hellyon (n.): Coined by the Netherworld agents, used to describe a disorderly, troublesome, rowdy or mischievous irregular, metaphysical or inhuman.

Journeyer (n): A member of Elysium, their purpose is to carry the innocents home, to Elysium, upon their death.

Kler'voient (adj): Having or exhibiting an ability to perceive events in the future or past, beyond normal sensory contact. *Kler'odient* (adj.) Having or exhibiting an ability to hear things no one else can hear.

The Netherworld (n.): A powerful government organization that polices the irregular, metaphysical or inhuman. They are seen as neither good nor evil. Their main focus is to eradicate the Rancor Order.

The Orygin (n.): The fountainhead of our existence, the leader of the Overworld, also known as 'God' in human cultures.

Proletaryans (adj.): A race of soulless animated corpses, under the command of the Rancor Order. They are controlled by the son of the Genesys.

Pergetore (n.): A place or state of suffering inhabited by the souls of sinners who are expiating their sins before going to Elysium.

Prophetyc (adj.): The prediction come true, the birthed child of an angel and demon. They are half in and half out of this world. Their soul is jailed in Pergetore, as part of a deal to keep balance between sides, until they have earned their wings. Their paths can be good or evil. They, like mankind, are given free will.

The Rancor Order (pr. n.): An order created to exterminate the irregular, metaphysical and inhuman.

The Reaping (v.): To harvest the life of a higher born Day Walkyr, ending their first life in the thirtieth year of their birth. An event held to celebrate the rebirthing of a Vampyre, The Reaping is generally held only by the noble, royal or higher born. The consequence for noncompliance with this tradition is a black smear on the family name, banishment from society and possible death.

The Rector (n.): The unknown leader of The Netherworld. Their identity is kept classified.

The Ruynous (n.): The chief evil spirit, the great adversary of humanity, the leader of Hades. Ruynous is also known as 'The Devil' in human cultures.

Seer (n.): A hybrid child from the line of a Sibyl. A seer is half Vampyre and half Sibyl. Through supernatural insight, they can see the past, present and future. Once missionaries, they disbanded when they realized their actions were interrupting the natural destiny of mankind. Seers have taken a vow to allow the natural flow of life to continue, acting only as fate dictates. They cannot see a future where their wicked intentions have altered destiny.

Slayers (n.): Trained assassins of The Genesys Project, who protect their race against the Rancor Order and the Genesys.

Spekter (n.): A ghoul, undead and reanimated corpse. Exits own grave when ground becomes unholy or disturbed.

Therianthropes (n.): Also known as shifters, weres, Lycans, Therian. Therianthropy is an infection of the blood, creating the ability to shift from human into animal or creature. This virus is highly contagious.

Tryhal (n): The examination of the facts before a tribunal, often including issues of law and customs, as well as those of fact. A tryhal is for the determination of a person's guilt or innocence by due process of law and customs. This ritual is to restore honor. All verdicts are final and generally fatal.

Vampyre (n.): A preternatural being, reanimated after the first death. Vampyre must drink the life force of a living being in order to survive. You cannot be turned into a Vampyre. This was part of your DNA. Upon your first death, you rise as a Vampyre.

The Vestalis Maxima (n): The chief Vestal Virgyn, who oversees the efforts of the Vestal Virgyns. The Vestalis Maxima is the most important high priestess. Vowed to chastity and service, they live a primarily solitary life, never to mate or marry, never to produce offspring. They are chosen from the original Vestal Virgyns. This duty cannot be relinquished. Their Reaping would mark the date of lifelong service to this honored position. Only true death itself can part them from their duties.

The Vestal Virgyns (n): Named after the virgins consecrated to Vesta, vowed to chastity, education and solidarity. Chosen only from the line of the Vestal Virgyns, they are committed to maintaining their virginity until the age of thirty. At the age of thirty, they complete The Reaping, their first-born lives harvested, their Day Walkyr life extinguished. They mate only with the Royal Line. A failed Vestal Virgyn is condemned, entombed, forced to starve to death.

Wardyn (n.): A key holder or gate keeper in the Underworld.

Watchyr (n.): A being from the Overworld, sent as guidance. They are unable to intervene in the paths of those under their charge.

More books from
L.A. Kennedy

Leading a fierce battle to protect his race, Cael must choose between the life he has and the woman he wants.

*There's war brewing and only one group of Slayers to
protect their race. Their second-in-command must choose
between the life he'd be forced to live
and the life he'd kill for.*

About the Author

L.A. Kennedy

L.A. Kennedy, beyond the story…

L.A. Kennedy is a Canadian born writer, living in the ever-growing city of Vancouver, Canada. Here, she spends her days getting lost in the beauty of reading and writing. L.A. Kennedy mainly writes fictional books. And can be found researching myth, folklore, and everything in between, with a special interest in edge-of-your-seat paranormal romance. L.A. Kennedy can be found behind a mountain of books, on any given Sunday.

L.A. Kennedy's writing credits include two hit series that mix mystery, horror, paranormal romance, fantasy, and intrigue.

L.A. Kennedy loves to hear from readers. You can find contact information, website details and an author profile page at https://www.totallybound.com/

Home of Erotic Romance

www.ingramcontent.com/pod-product-compliance
Lightning Source LLC
Chambersburg PA
CBHW022125170626
46808CB00002B/843